THE BACHELOR'S WIFE

SMALL TOWN BACHELORS

SUSAN WARNER

EG PUBLISHING

This is a work of fiction. Similarities to real people, places, or events are entirely coincidental.

THE BACHELOR'S WIFE

First Edition. September 28, 2022.

Copyright © 2022 EG Publishing

ISBN: 978-1-953834-73-7

Written by Susan Warner.

If you like to get a free book from Susan Warner and would like to join her Newsletter sign up here Susan's newsletter

CHAPTER 1

*G*rayson Chance had given up on hope at the age of five. No one would have blamed him. He was a three-year resident at the Boy's home in Westchester, NY. He had been told by many that if he wasn't adopted in the first year, he was going to have to go into a lot of foster homes. He might get lucky and find a family that wanted him, but it wasn't likely.

That was the same year that he met Patti Chance. It was the year that he discovered hope again and the year his life changed. He had to admit, he hadn't made it easy for Patti. In fact, he had done everything he could for her to return him back to the orphanage. He had learned his lesson about getting comfortable at a foster home only to have them take him back.

Patti was a round, robust woman who had a smile on her face no matter the time of day. When Grayson asked her why she was smiling, she told him she was waiting to see what wonders he would surprise her with next.

For the next four months he pushed as hard as he could to get Patti to take him back, but to no avail. She had withstood it all and no matter what, she had kept him and loved him. It was because of that tenacity and open heart that Grayson had a hard time understanding the telephone call that had come from his sister Kendra. She was saying the only mother he had ever known, Patti, had passed away from heart complications that he hadn't even known about.

Grayson sat in the lawyer's office and thought over all Patti had done for him. She had given him her last name and made him feel like family. She had taught him that it was better to give than to receive. Patti had always told him the truth, and until today he would have said they had no secrets. When he had asked her what he could be when he grew up, Patti didn't pull any punches, she told him and his brothers what she saw.

"Gray, you have the gift of gab. You could probably talk a desert dweller into buying premium sand. Find something where that skill will help you help others, and you'll always feel fulfilled."

"Filled with what momma Patti?" a young Grayson had asked. Patti had just laughed and patted him on the head.

"You'll see Gray, you'll see."

As a result, Grayson participated in the debate team in school, and then marketing and advertising. He learned about Cialdini's six principles of persuasion. It spoke of reciprocity, doing for others with no strings attached and what others would like to do for you. Scarcity, the less there is of it, the more people want it. Be Authoritative, people like to do what authoritative people say. People will commit and be consistent with their perceived self-image. The last two were liking and social proof. It turns out that people are more likely to follow people they like if a lot of people are doing it.

All of the principles in the world didn't help him now because the one person he would have needed to persuade to tell him about her condition was gone. Patti was gone.

Grayson sat in the worn leather chair in front of the lawyer. The eagle-eyed man gave Grayson another look, and it took all Grayson had in him to not to shift in his seat under the scrutiny. He didn't like lawyers. Lawyers never delivered good news. A lawyer had delivered him to the boy's home when he was younger and now a lawyer was about to read to him the last wishes of his mother. Patti wasn't his birth mother, but she had earned the title as far as Grayson was concerned.

The smell of furniture polish permeated the air. It was as if all the items had been staged for the moment. Tomes lay about on his desk as if the lawyer read them. How much reading did it take to deliver bad news all the time? The walls were decorated with degrees earned and conferred honorarily upon him. It looked impressive but when Grayson remembered why he was here, all of the documents mean nothing.

"I don't want to rush you Mr. Dane but I wasn't privy to my mother's will, and I'd like to catch up with my sister today and go over whatever she needs help with, as well as be there for her during this time of grief for our family."

The lawyer nodded sagely and then began to shuffle the papers on the desk around as if they have somehow changed in the last hour. He looked up at Grayson and the empty seat next to him and then back at the papers.

Grayson began to think the lawyer isn't so bright after all.

"I guess I'm still not clear on why the will couldn't be sent to us all via email since she's already been buried, and we were willing to comply with the terms of her will regarding who should get the house."

Mr. Dane nods again and then grunts.

"Mr. Chance, I don't know if you were aware, but Patti and I went way back. We knew each other when she was married. I was there when she received the news about her husband dying in 'Nam. I say this so you'll understand my familiarity with her."

Grayson shifted in his seat. This wasn't going the way he thought it would at all.

"Patti was a family person and she decided that she wanted her house to go to the first person who showed up."

Grayson smiled.

"That doesn't seem so difficult, as I'm already here."

Mr. Dane nodded his head.

"She wanted to ensure that you were on the right path, you see. She left me a note saying you'd be the first one to show up and it turns out she knew you all well."

Grayson smiled. Of course, she knew he would be here first. He was always the one to get the news from Kendra and then he would update his brothers. Also, out of all of the brothers, the home he grew up in was the one thing he had ever wanted to save from his childhood. He had already talked about it with his other brothers, and they had agreed he could have the house and keep the foster care program running as well if he wanted to. For Grayson, it wasn't just a house, it was a safe haven. So yes, he was here first to make sure it was taken care of. However, there was a stalling that was going on that Grayson sensed in Mr. Dane that something unexpected and very mom-like was about to happen. The little shadow of fear manifested when Mr. Dane said she wanted the best for them.

"She knew us better than we knew ourselves," Grayson murmured.

When Mr. Dane smiled, Grayson gave him a sideway glance and prepared for the other shoe to drop.

"I'm so glad you agree that she knew you well. This is why she also made the stipulation that you could move in with your wife."

The other shoe hadn't just dropped, it had slammed to the ground. Mr. Dane hadn't moved, so much for it being lawyer humor. A wife. Okay, it was true he was thirty-eight and he had told Patti that he'd be married by thirty-seven. Grayson wanted to roll his eyes when he remembered he hadn't told Patti that he had broken up with Sheila, his latest girlfriend. The reason they had separated was that he wanted a wife who would stay home with their kids for at least the first six months. Sheila thought the idea was archaic and walked out. It didn't matter they had been engaged for a year and he had been telling her this from the beginning. In the end, Sheila's answer was she thought he would grow out of it.

"Well, I don't have a wife… yet," Grayson said. "I mean I will have one but just not now."

Mr. Dane frowned as Grayson stammered. Grayson can see this is not going to be a quick laugh and we move on.

"I'm afraid that the conditions to get the house were very specific."

Grayson clenched his jaw in a perfect smile. It was the smile he gives donors who are on the fence about donating to his charity.

"I completely understand your position. I think we got off on the wrong foot. I'm not married now but I'm engaged. We were trying to work things out to get the family together and … you know."

Mr. Dane shook his head.

"Actually, I don't know," Mr. Dane said drolly.

Grayson kept his smile in place and started mentally scrolling through all of the women he knew that he could call, and they wouldn't mind being a stand-in fiancée on the phone or maybe making one public appearance.

"Well, what I'm trying to say is my fiancée didn't come here today as I didn't know she would be required," Grayson said, "but I can assure you that she would be able to confirm our plans." Grayson kept his smile in place and waited for Mr. Dane's next move. He kept eye contact, looked sincere, and tried not to crowd the desk so he doesn't appear threatening. This wasn't Grayson's first rodeo.

Mr. Dane closed the papers in front of him and then gave Grayson a smile. Mr. Dane pulled out a drawer and produced a key. Grayson didn't want to sigh in relief, but he was glad the lawyer was going to be reasonable. Perhaps this encounter would change the way Grayson viewed lawyers.

"Here is the key to the house. You can get settled and invite your fiancé. I understand you didn't know the terms of Patti's will so your fiancé couldn't be here. Also, having a wedding so close to a tragedy doesn't seem like the way to go, either."

Grayson nodded his head and took the key.

"Thank you for being so understanding. My fiancé and I appreciate the compassion you've shown us today." Grayson pulled the key towards himself and a piece of him clicks into place. The world is right and then he hears Mr. Dane clear his throat.

"I do understand and appreciate your situation, which is why I'm going to allow you some latitude. I've given you the key, but we won't sign the deed over to you until I meet your fiancé and I'm comfortable that all is the way it should be."

Grayson wondered how long a person could really survive if their heart stopped. Certainly, they would just keel over to the side and expire. He was waiting for that to happen to him but there was no darkness clouding his vision, no light in the sky and no angelic voices in the background.

"Excuse me?"

Mr. Dane gathered up the papers on his desk.

"I think when I meet your fiancé and spend a little time with her, I'll feel better that the intent that Patti had for you is being fulfilled."

"Of course," Grayson said. Then Mr. Dane stood up, and Grayson followed him.

"Do you know when your fiancé will be here?"

Grayson shakes his head no and that is the first truth about his mystery fiancé he has said. He's going through his list again and now knows he will have to call his brothers if he plans on doing this.

"I'll reach out to her and see what her availability is."

"Great plan. I think this all falls right into Patti's plan. She wanted you to be happy and knew how important the house and family were to you."

"Umm, you don't say," Grayson commented as he followed the lawyer out of his office and into the waiting area that is empty.

Mr. Dane pats Grayson on his shoulder and gives him a smile.

"I know this would have put a smile on Patti's face. I can't wait to meet the little woman," Mr. Dane said as he directed Grayson to the elevator. Grayson kept his smile in place and just nodded. When the doors closed, he leaned against the elevator wall. He also wondered to himself who would be his mystery fiancé.

"I can't wait to meet the little woman myself," Grayson said to himself as the elevator doors opened.

CHAPTER 2

*R*ose Sallow understood that life wasn't fair or unfair, it just was. She didn't always have that thought but after the birth of her identical twin girls, her worldview changed. She had six years with her husband before he died. Her husband had complained of a mild headache that had become a migraine and then two days later he was in the hospital slipping into a coma that he never awoke from. Some people would rail against the world. In fact, she was a part of those people for about a year. Then it came to her that she was angry about not having more time. She looked at her twins who had less than five years with her ex.

Her husband Edward and herself had opened the cleaning business and decided it would be for their kids. It was one of the few decisions they had both agreed on. Edward wouldn't be here to help her raise the kids, but he'd be there in spirit. Rose would make sure that she preserved their legacy gift from their father.

Lately, she had been wishing Edward was with her in more than just spirit. A few days ago, she had been contacted by Jonathan Castle. He claimed he was a friend and a business associate of Edward's. Rose disregarded that thought because she and Edward shared everything about the business. They had saved for the business. Both of them worked double shifts and jobs and finally when they had enough money, they opened up the business. She didn't know what kind of game Mr. Castle was running but he wasn't going to do it with her.

The girls were at her best friend's house, Traci Baker. Traci had a little girl, Sophia, and all of the children got along. Traci and she took turns watching the kids and sometimes Portia did, too. Although Portia Morales would never admit to it, it was the unspoken secret that Portia liked watching the kids. Traci and Rose knew Portia's secret but there was something that not even four years of them being "the trio of life" would get Portia to loosen her tongue and let them know why she was in denial about such an obvious truth.

The trio of life is what they called themselves. Portia had never had kids and claimed she never would. She was the one untouched by marriage. Traci had a daughter and husband that Portia contemplated nefarious ends daily for the husband. Last, Rose had been married to the love of her life. Then he had been taken away from her just when they are about to enjoy a family and a new business finally out of the red. So they were the maiden, the mother and widow respectively. Together they joked they made the trio of life.

Patti Chance had passed away and she was one

of Rose's favorite customers. Her granddaughter had let her keep the key to the house and this afternoon she had decided to come by and do her weekly cleaning. There was almost nothing to do since no one was living in the house now. Rose loved the house. She could imagine her twin girls running through here. The house was better than the one-room starter she and Edward had bought. She remembered arguing with him that they would outgrow the house, but Edward had insisted it would be cozy. It was a pleasure to clean Patti's house but so sad about the circumstance. She hoped the new owner appreciated it and didn't do something crazy like tear it down to put up some art deco motif.

When her phone rang she jumped after being pulled out of her reverie. The screen read SPAM RISK. She knew it was Jonathan again. He was like a dog with a bone and not in a good way. No way would he leave her alone. Rose decided she needed to face this head on. She'd let him talk and then it would be over.

"Okay, go ahead and tell me your story," Rose said.

"Rose?" Rebecca Price's voice comes through. "Rose Sallow?" Rose closed her eyes and wondered if her luck could get any worse. She leaned against the door jamb of the house and tried to find her nice voice without too much pleading coming through. Rebecca was one of the connections she had made through Patti, and Rebecca had been very helpful in getting her other jobs at group foster homes in the area. It was true that Rose had to travel a bit further than she wanted to some of them, but steady money was more important and pushed her company into the black.

"I'm sorry Ms. Price. The number was unknown on my phone, and I thought it was someone else who I'm expecting a call from." Although, as many times as she had told him she wouldn't talk to him, maybe that wasn't the most logical thought that he would call either.

"It's no worry, a single mother has a lot on her mind. I wanted to talk to you and maybe help take some of the pressure off of you."

"Ah, okay," Rose said. She wasn't sure what the conversation would be about, but she couldn't afford to say no. She looked down at her dirty jeans and stained tee shirt and hoped Portia was home to give her some clothing options.

"Good, I'm thinking we can do an early dinner in about two hours. We can meet at Uncle Peter's and the dress is business casual. See you there." Rebecca didn't even wait to hear if Rose will make it. When Rose heard the dial tone, she knows she'll have to make an emergency stop at Portia's. She quickly dials her and murmurs to herself, "please, please."

"Hello, sugar. Have you decided you want to know what the other side does when they have no children?" Portia teased.

"No, I need some business casual clothing in two hours and I'm at Patti Chance's house."

"Come to me sister. My walk-in closets are waiting for you," Portia said with a laugh.

~

Thirty minutes later, Rose was at Portia's door. When Portia opened the door and saw her attire, she shook her head.

"It doesn't matter what you were doing, I can't think of a single reason you should look like this on your day off from working," Portia scolded.

Rose wanted to say something, but what could she say? She couldn't say 'She was feeling nostalgic and went in to clean a nice woman's house who passed away.' Portia would lecture her on having her heart on her sleeve.

"Portia, lecture later, clothing now, please."

"Okay, what did she say?"

"Business casual," Rose said as she nibbled on her bottom lip. The first outfit Portia brought out was a black bustier, black pants and a short red jacket. Rose scrunched up her brow and shook her head.

"What kind of business casual is that?"

Portia smiled. "This look said I could pay for dinner but you're treating."

Rose rolled her eyes. "Portia, business casual with a woman."

"Oh, and the venue again?"

"Uncle Peter's," Rose said.

"Ah, that is important. So, let's go with basic black pants so you are comfortable. I think I have a cream top in here, as well as a sporty jacket that has rolled-up sleeves to the elbow."

"I met her through Patti, and I don't want her to look at me and think what a loser this woman is, she must have been one of Patti's charity cases," Rose bemoaned.

"I think you are way too hard on yourself.

Everyone loves you and sees how hard you work," Portia said over her shoulder as she dug through her closet.

"Well, I don't think she wants to talk to me to say that she's admired me from afar. In any case, I'm not going to know the answer if we can't find some clothing for me. Portia, I'm grateful but I need to get to Uncle Peter's. Can we hurry up, please?"

"Of course. I have just the ensemble but it's at the bottom of the closet. I figured I'd never use it."

Rose's eyebrows lifted in skepticism.

"You've never worn this, but you think it's going to work for me? I don't know .." Rose said hesitantly.

Portia stood up with the items in her hands and a smile on her face.

"Don't worry. I just don't go out to business casual places with women, but I have an outfit just in case, "Portia said wiggling her eyebrows with a smile on her face.

"Okay, let's see the full effect," Rose said as Portia went to lay out the outfit on her bed. Rose looked at the ensemble and thought it would be great if she could be as confident as the outfit was. "I'm hoping I can wear this. It looked like something that goes on a ..."

Portia interrupted her. "It's something that goes on a strong, confident woman who raises two daughters and ran a business. You are so right! Put it on Rose. This is your inner Rose you haven't embraced yet, but I know she's in there. Besides, clothing can give you confidence like nothing else can."

Rose picked up the outfit and scrambled into Portia's bathroom. When Rose came out and saw herself in the full-length mirror Portia has in her bedroom, she looked like a different woman."

"Oh yes, that is the inner power woman I am waiting to see emerge," Portia said.

Rose wanted to naysay her but looking at her reflection she could almost believe Portia when she spun her tales.

"Okay Cinderella, you don't need to worry about getting back home, the outfit is yours to keep. Besides, it looked like it looked way better on you than I ever imagined it on me. You've just got to tell me what the news was that warranted you getting taken out."

Rose looked at herself one more time still in wonder.

"I wonder what it is, as well," Rose said as she looked at her watch, then ran to hug Portia before heading toward the door.

Rose got into her blue car and then tried to think of what it was that Rebecca could want to discuss with her. Through the last year, Rebecca had given her name as a reference but when that had happened they never needed to meet. She knew Rebecca was the head of several private foster homes. Maybe she wanted to set up an exclusive contract? Having steady money would be a great thing for budgeting but she'd have to find a permanent solution for the girls. Did she really want to find someone else to pick up her girls? Since Edward's passing, she had tried to spend as much time with the girls as possible. Rose wanted to make sure they felt secure. Could she really think about leaving them now that school was going to start, and their time would already be cut short by this new phase they would start next month. Could she say no to the money and working to save for the girl's future?

Before she realized it, she was out of her blue geo metro. She knew people looked at her car and made jokes about how the car didn't run on an engine but squirrels that she fed under the hood. Rose didn't care at all; it was what she could afford, and it got the job done. As Rose took a couple of steps, who should she see standing in front of Uncle Peter's but the last person she wanted to see ever. If it weren't for bad luck she'd have no luck at all, Rose thought. She thought about turning back to her car but in the moment of indecision, Jonathan Castle spotted her. Rose wasn't one to run from whatever life dished out and she wasn't going to start now. Throwing back her shoulders and breathing through her lips so no one could see, she stepped forward to meet the enemy.

"Rose, I didn't know you'd be here," he said. Rose wanted to say 'really' as it seemed like he knew every other place she'd be. However, he had a woman on his arm, and she looked mildly annoyed already. Rose didn't have the heart to make anyone uncomfortable or put them in a worse position. She didn't want to make the woman on his arm any more uncomfortable.

She looked at Jonathan Castle and tried to process the enemy before her. He was a well-built man. He had the beard all the men were sporting, and his eyes were blue like a block of ice. He claimed he knew Edward. It wouldn't have surprised Rose if that were true but the rest of the story he was trying to pitch was too much. He wanted her to believe that

Edward and him were business partners and all the good looked in the world wouldn't get her to believe such a story.

"I'm here on a business meeting." Rose tried to sound as cool and professional as she knew she looked. Then the woman by his side spoke up.

"You don't look like you're hurting for anything," the woman said sourly. Rose didn't know where the comment had come from or why, but she didn't have time for either of them.

"I can see the business is doing well by you Rose." The way Jonathan looked over Rose made her straighten her spine. She didn't know what it was with the two of them, but she wasn't going to be bullied by anyone. "We need to talk about the business and what needs to be done," Jonathan pushed.

Rose pursed her lips and sighed.

"Listen, I will listen to what you have to say so we can be done. However, that conversation won't be happening tonight."

"Edward always did say you set the tone. I can see he was right. I've left my number in the message on your phone. Give me a call tomorrow, that's the latest I can wait."

Rose gave them both a nod and then walked into the restaurant. She wasn't sure what Rebecca was going to say but whatever it was, she was sure she could handle it ten times better than whatever it was that Jonathan was going to say to her tomorrow.

CHAPTER 3

*G*rayson hadn't wanted to come out tonight. He didn't understand why women had to discuss everything in restaurants with large price tags. As soon as he had left Mr. Dane's office, he called Kendra to confirm if the caveat in the will was true. After a long two-hour conversation on why people shouldn't try to manipulate others was over, Grayson was in the same predicament. He needed to produce a fiancé in order to get the home he had always dreamed of owning.

He had to admit at one point he had thought he had the love of his life and would bring her to Inheritance Bay. Then again, if he were honest he'd realize that Sheila wasn't the love of his life. He was just tired of looking. Grayson hadn't been able to stay in a relationship for longer than eight months. In the end it all boiled down to the idea that he wanted to be with someone who wanted to grow old with him, talk to him and maybe even help him in his job of helping charities raise money. The women liked the money he made now. They appreciated his investments, and he knew he was an attractive man but then they spoke about traveling the world and meeting all of the stars of the famous charities and the relationship started to sour for him. He didn't even want to think about the times he had brought up Inheritance Bay and they had politely listened and then patted his knee saying they understood that he had escaped Inheritance Bay. How the idea of not going back was probably his motivation. When he met Sheila she was pleasant, attractive and wanted to get married. Grayson thought that was his last chance at love, so he grabbed on to it and tried to make it work. Instead of being rewarded for his efforts, he was sitting in an expensive restaurant waiting for an actress who had agreed to be his fake fiancé, if they could come to some agreement.

Grayson arrived early hoping to see the woman who said she would be all in black with something red on it. At first, he thought she was trying to be funny. She touted being discreet but in Inheritance Bay, if a woman wore red everyone would know by morning. That told him that this woman wasn't from Inheritance Bay which was a relief in and of itself. He didn't want any complications to this charade.

When Gray walked in everyone was already paired up. He went to stand by the bar and watch the front door. After five minutes he was aggravated looking for this mystery woman. He started to rethink the plan, but he didn't see any other options. He was on his second tonic water when the doors decorated with fall leaves and a Styrofoam horn of goods heralding the beginning of fall and the coming of Thanksgiving were thrown open by a woman who was magnificent.

She had pushed the doors open but was waiting to stop them from slamming and in that moment Grayson thought this wasn't going to be so bad after all. She was a contradiction dressed in a black pant outfit and sleeves rolled to her elbows and then gingerly holding out her hands as to not disturb anyone, as if her presence alone wouldn't be enough. He saw her lean her head toward the hostess presumably to give her name. He hadn't given his, so there was no way for her to know he was already there. He saw her look around and then find a seat on the far end of the bar.

"Well, you certainly know how to make an entrance," he said. Instead of seeing her look up at him so he can finally see what color her eyes are, she doesn't even budge from her phone, which she is scrolling through messages.

"Thank you but no thank you," she replies distracted.

"It's hard on a man's ego that he couldn't get you to look up from text messages for you to tell him to go away. I know I've been out of the game for a while, but I have to say you make me think I'm either way rustier than I thought or I've been around kind woman who understand that I have tender feelings."

She looked up from the screen and if Grayson thought her entrance was captivating, it didn't hold a candle to her gaze. Her eyes were almond-shaped and silky brown. They were the type of brown that had layers and you wanted to stare at them for a while until you figured them all out. A few moments later, I saw the questioning look enter her eyes and then she began to nibble on her bottom lip.

"I wouldn't have placed you as having tender feelings. I'm going to take a guess that with your looked you probably get more than your fair share of attention to find someone who will believe you might have those tender feelings."

Grayson smiled. He can't remember the last time a woman said what she was thinking to him, and he had to admit it was refreshing and engaging all at the same time.

"Well, the good news is you think I'm attractive. I think we may need to work on the thinking I'm shallow and need validation but if that's what it takes to pull your attention away from the phone, I'll take it for now."

She laughed and it was husky and deep. It wasn't one of those polite laugh's women perfect, instead, it was one that said it was all her and unpracticed.

"I can see how this wounded creature thing might work for you but you're selling yourself short."

"Whew! I'm glad you said that because I have to say my confidence was dropping as you spoke but that little pick me up will help me get through the night."

"I don't want to be the cause of an evening gone wrong. Let me tell you there is nothing wrong with you at all and I'm waiting for someone who hasn't shown yet, so I was hoping to answer some messages before they arrived."

"Work messages before a date?" he asked.

She shrugged. "If I were independently wealthy maybe I would be different but I'm an independent business owner, so I have to make sure I follow up on all the leads, say thank you for new opportunities and offer great service to those who trust me to do their work."

All Grayson could hear was she was perfect. All of his doubts about hiring an actress went out the door. Not only was it a great idea, but he had also stumbled upon the best person ever.

"I have to say that is a great work ethic. You're waiting for someone?"

She gave him a once over.

"If I weren't waiting for someone, I would have to tell I was for safety's sake. You do need to work on your approach. It's the age of gorgeous men are doing crazy things."

Grayson quickly held up his hand and then took out his wallet and opened it to his driver's license.

"You're right. You can ask anyone in town to vouch for me. My name is Grayson Chance."

"Chance? As in one of Patti's boys?" she asked.

When she mentioned Patti, Grayson went on alert. Maybe she wasn't as perfect as he thought.

"How do you know my mom? Is this some sort of setup and – "

"Hold on cowboy. It's true you look good and now that I know you are one of Patti's boys I can see how you might be suspicious of all things, but my name is Rose Sallow, okay?"

Grayson made his career and money remembering names and he didn't know that one. It must have shown on his face because the woman who was a little shy coming in the door was getting angry and he could see it building in her like how a small wind tunnel picks up the strength to become a funnel and grow into a tornado.

"Of course, you don't know my name because you don't pay the bills to keep the house maintained. I usually deal with your sister Kendra."

"What does Kendra need with an actress?"

The woman looked at him confused.

"I don't know, but since I'm the cleaning service that made sure the house is together, I've never asked outside of my realm about the other things she may need."

"You're the cleaning service? I thought you were here to meet someone."

"I am Romeo," then the woman looked at her phone and then turns to look at the door to the restaurant which has just closed. There is a short woman with black hair looking around, "the person I'm here to meet just walked in."

Grayson looked at the woman and then sighed in bewilderment. Right before he answers he gets a text. SORRY, CAN'T DO TONIGHT, A GIG CAME UP, LETS RESCHDULE. Now it became clear that this woman isn't the one he was supposed to meet but she is the one he needs.

"Listen, I'm sorry I made a lot of assumptions and I know you have to go but can I get your number so we can meet up."

She stands up and Grayson is thrilled to see she is just a couple of inches shorter than him. She'll fit under his arm perfectly.

"Listen, I'm not giving you my number. You've already admitted your insecure. You approach women in bars as if you know them and I work for you technically. All of the reasons not to see you."

"Rose, there you are," the dark-haired woman from the front said as she gets closer. Instead of me being able to defend myself, Rose takes the opportunity to go to her dinner date and left Grayson at the bar rethinking his situation. Grayson didn't believe in luck or coincidence. The night didn't go the way he planned but it did pan out to be what he needed. He just needed to find a way to get Rose Sallow on board.

CHAPTER 4

*R*ose was happy and sad to leave Grayson at the bar. If she were honest with herself, she'd have to admit she enjoyed his conversation way too much. It felt odd and freeing to banter with a man. Rebecca was already chattering, and Rose had to get her head in the game to understand what the reason was they were here. Rebecca walked over to a table where a man was already looking at the menu and drinking what looked like lemonade.

Just when Rose was about to tap Rebecca on the shoulder she turned around.

"Rose, I'd like you to meet my husband Anders."

Rose held out her hand and hoped the confusion didn't show on her face.

"It's a pleasure to meet you. I've worked with your wife and she's a joy."

Anders laughed.

"You are very kind, but you don't need to be. Rebecca can be like a dog with a bone, but she believes in what she does. Running the foster homes made us both happy. It's the reason we are both here tonight. We both love the way you care and maintained the houses you've worked on for us. You have an eye not just for cleaning but house maintenance that can easily be overlooked. Having you point out those things has also brought the issue to our attention that we need someone to take care of the houses, as well as do general maintenance. We've decided to hire someone to do that, as we are looking to expand and know this will only become a larger issue if left unaddressed."

Rose wasn't sure about anything anymore. She thought this meeting was about getting more business, but it seems it's about getting rid of her.

"I am glad for the both of you. It seems like your good fortune isn't so much for me."

Rebecca laughed.

"My husband is the best when it comes to numbers but otherwise he's a work in progress," Rebecca said as she placed her hand over Anders as she scooted closer to him on the bench. Rose looked on. "What my husband hasn't gotten around to saying is we would like you to run the department that manages the maintenance and cleaning of our foster homes. We have fifteen now and will be adding six more by the end of this year and we have future projections, as well."

Rose looked at them both and when the waitress comes to take the order and reads off the specials, Rose nods her head and said, "number two please." For a moment the excitement and the joy that someone else has acknowledged her work and accomplishment made her feel ecstatic and then it hits her what this really means.

"Is this a part-assignment?" Rose asked even though Rose knows the answer. Rebecca and Anders look at one another before Rebecca shakes her head in denial.

"No Rose, it's not. This would be a full-time position that would require all of your time in the beginning."

"I'm so sorry I can't accept this position."

Anders shakes his head and gives a dollar to Rebecca.

"You know, Rebecca told me you would say that. I told her you would jump at this opportunity"

Rose looked to Rebecca hoping she would be able to help her out. Taking a big sigh Rebecca turned to Anders.

"Anders, I told you that Rebecca has a business that she and her late husband started together. She ran it by herself."

Anders looked at Rose and sighed. "I can't say that I understand the emotional attachment to the business. I can say that I understand what it's like to love someone to distraction," he said squeezing Rebecca's hand. "However, I also know that when you love someone you don't want them to run themselves in the ground. Running a business alone and being a single parent can't be easy."

"You're right, running the business and being a mom isn't easy, but I want to preserve this company for my daughters. It's the last thing their father and I created and one day I'd like to pass it on to them, if they want it."

Anders took a sip of his drink and then looked at Rose long and hard.

"I have to say that I'm truly impressed by your

morality and hopes for your children. Your loyalty to your husband's memory is also commendable. What I think you're missing is the bigger picture. The consistent pay and the opportunities you'll be able to offer your girls now. The chance to spend more time with them and not have to worry about childcare. Rebecca told me the girls were getting ready for school. That can be a trying time for children. If you took this job you'd have set hours and we'd be more than accommodating when it comes to your children. As a single business owner, I don't think you're going to find that flexibility."

Rose wanted to scream at him and at Rebecca. She knew what he was saying was probably right, but they hadn't known Edward and she couldn't shake it that she owed it to Edward to do this.. They didn't understand passing dreams on to the girls or trying to provide a good image of their father.

"I do understand how hard being alone can be. It's not like your offer isn't tempting."

Rebecca cleared her throat.

"Rose, Anders hasn't mentioned to you that you'll set this department up as your own. You'll be able to have staff as soon as you can hire them."

Rose looked at Rebecca and she had to blink back the tears that were threatening to fall. To have staff and be able to train others and be with the girls was a dream of hers. If she kept on the track she was on, she might be able to do that in about six years, if all of her contacts were steady and the growth was consistent. To have that right now would be... bliss.

"Look Rose, I can tell that you are torn. I don't want you to give a final answer now. Think on it and then get back to me."

Rose nodded her head and the evening continued on in a fog. There was polite conversation and a lot of nodding to stories that Rose would never be able to recall. It was like slogging through the water. No matter how fast she might want the evening to go, it went at its own time.

Somewhere after dinner and while they were enjoying dessert, Rebecca spoke on the plans to expand the homes and how they were going to have so many expanded services. All of their plans just emphasized how she was being left behind by sticking to her guns. It made her re-think if this is what Edward would have wanted. All the while she kept a smile on her face. She wasn't sure who was more eager to leave, her or Anders.

Standing at the door Anders held out his hand.

"It was amazing meeting a woman of such strong convictions. I hope you give our offer some consideration. I'm the last one to talk about anything emotional but I'd want you to make the best decision for those little girls who are with you."

"I will and thank you so much for thinking of me."

Rose watched them walk off to valet and she began to walk to her car that was parked nearby as Anders words rolled around in her head.

"Rose!" a voice called out and she turned to see if Anders was going to make one last pitch, although the voice sounded familiar it wasn't Anders. It was her boss who looked too good waving her down. Now that Rose could see him in all of his glory, she had to admit that he was well put together and that was all the more reason she shouldn't be talking to him about anything but cleaning.

"Tell me how is it that you are here, at this time?" she asked.

"I wanted it to be that we naturally met outside of the place that we were both eating but I was stood up for the evening, so I had dinner alone and couldn't get you off of my mind."

"Really?"

Grayson smiled and if she wasn't mistaken, Rose could swear there was a slight blush on his face.

"It's partially true. I was stood up tonight. I did eat here alone. However, I did wait for you by the entrance. I saw you with Rebecca and I didn't want to come over since the conversation could have been personal or intense."

Rose shook her head and then crossed her arms over her chest. Grayson had the kind of charm that any woman would love to be showered in. He was the man that every mother hoped her daughter would run into and they would live happily ever after. The problem here was that Rose had already done this before. She had already been someone's happily ever after, and that person had left her. Rose understood that life moved on, but she wasn't sure she wanted to risk and trust like that again. The pain never went away, you just learned to live with it.

"You know my name. You have my number, what else is it that you are looking for here?"

"I have all of those things and you didn't give me any of them. I know I haven't presented the best front here but I don't want to be that pest of a guy who can't take a hint. I'd like to go out with you. Any place you want. I understand I might have come on a little strong but I just wanted to show you I was interested. The most important thing is to make sure you are comfortable. Without your say so to go forward this can stop here and I'll be glad that I met you at all."

Rose looked at him and decided he was safe enough. He's her employer. She's not looking for any type of relationship, but it would satisfy the trio if she went on a date with a man.

"A new place called Claw's lobster house opened in Trailblazer Park. I hear they bring the food to you on the benches." Rose deliberately picked the most public place she could find, and he smiled back at her as if he knew.

"Are you sure you don't want to go catch them yourself and then steam them fresh?" he asked.

"Um like never!" Rose replied.

"Okay, I'll meet you there for lunch, you can text me when you are on your way." With that, he turns and walks to the restaurant. Rose can't help but have the last word.

"Grayson, how will you know where I am in the park?"

He turns and flashes her a smile that made her hold her breath in anticipation.

"It'll be easy to find the most beautiful woman in the park. See you tomorrow."

Rose can't believe the statement and how silly it was. Still, no matter how corny it was, Rose smiled all the way to her car thinking about Grayson.

CHAPTER 5

*R*ose looked at her twins in their bed asleep. After two stories and questions about school she was exhausted. She needed to let Portia know what happened, but Rose wasn't ready to share. The offer had shaken her in ways that she thought couldn't be done. Rose was sure it was a temporary shakiness, but it was still there. It was indecision and Rose hated it.

Rose picked up her phone and decided to get this conversation out of the way.

"Portia."

"It's about time you called. I know you've got the girls already, so I was wondering what was taking you so long. Now come on and spill it. What was the big deal about tonight going to such an expensive place?"

"They wanted to tell me that they were expanding and there would be more opportunities for me."

"Ooh, more opportunities? I'm liking the way

that sounds. What I really hear you saying is there's going to be more money somewhere."

Rose smiled to herself and knew that if she had told Portia the whole story, Portia would be on her way to her house.

"Money isn't everything."

"That's true. It's not everything. However, I'm going to have to say it is the beginning of getting most things."

Rose was sitting on her couch and becoming more uncomfortable as this situation went on. What she needed to do was to distract her friend.

"Well, besides talking to Rebecca, I also met a man."

"You what? You should have started with that one."

"He's not a new man. His name is Grayson."

"As in one of the Chance boys?"

"Well, he's not a boy. He's grown up into a well put together man."

"How well put together?" Portia asked as she lowered her voice an octave.

"He speaks in full sentences, doesn't drag his knuckles and didn't ask for references on my character or religion," Rose responded while rolling her eyes.

"I know you think I'm being picky and nosey in your life. However, I want to make sure that you get to move on. Edward wouldn't want you to mourn him forever. Now that we have that public service message out of the way, did you see any of his brothers with him?"

"You've got to be kidding me?" Rose asked laughing.

"Everyone in Inheritance Bay knows that somehow, even though they're not blood related, every one of the Chance brothers are drop dead gorgeous."

"Well, I wasn't looking for them. And everyone must not agree because he said he had been stood up for the night. Now, I'm not going to stay on here forever. I need to get some rest. Traci is going to pick up the girls tomorrow and now I need to get some administrative duties done. The boring part of owning your own business."

"Well, good job. On all fronts. I'll talk to you tomorrow."

The next day as Rose was matching up invoices, the doorbell rang. Rose looked around the room trying to see if the girls had left something they needed for pre-k. This is what happens when you try to work from home instead of going into the small office she rented. She didn't spot anything as she goes to the door and when she opens it, there is the last person Rose wants to see, Jonathan Castle. He gives Rose a tentative smile.

"I waited until the girls were gone. I didn't want you to be upset and I didn't want to upset them by talking about Edward," Jonathan said unsure but determined.

Rose wasn't happy to see Jonathan, but she knew that this has to be done. In a small way, she's happy that he had the decency to wait, maybe this encounter wouldn't be so bad after all.

"This time is as good as any, come in." Rose closed the door and walked him to her office where she was doing invoices. She was going to keep this as business focused as possible.

"So, I see you turned the TV room into your office," Jonathan said looking around the room. Rose tried not to be alarmed that he knew what the room was like before. It's the little clues that he seemed to know that caused the trepidation that she felt around him. It was times like this that made her question if Edward had told her everything. "I'm glad that you decided to talk to me. I don't want to take up a lot of your time and I know you don't want me here. The reason I'm here is because Edward borrowed a lot of money in order to start the business that you're running right now. I gave it to him as a loan and he gave me a share of the business as collateral."

The words hit her soul like small daggers, making little incisions that she couldn't fix.

"You want to be a partner in the business?" she asked tentatively.

Jonathan shook his head. "I've never had interest in running a business or even being a part of one. Edward was my frat buddy, and when he asked me for the money, and I had it, of course I gave it to him. I'm not interested in running a business at all. What I need right now is my money back. So, I'm not sure if you can go ahead and take a loan out for my half or if you can buy me out, but whatever it is, I need to get my portion of the money back."

Rose was reeling from every statement as if she were in a sea and rolls of waves kept crashing over her. Each wave moved her a little farther from the land and threatened to pull her under. This was no time for her to seize up with useless tears or cries of frustration.

"Do you have any proof or legal documentation? I would need something besides your word, and I need to know how much money we're talking about," Rose said in a voice that shocked her on how steady it was. Jonathan pulled out some paperwork from his sports coat and handed it to her. Rose looked it over and went straight to the back of the document to find Edward's scrawl on it. Seeing his handwriting made her throat go dry. Rose would always tease Edward that he never had to worry about anyone forging his signature because there were days Edward couldn't read his own signature. From that point she turned to the front page to read what Edward had done. She was on the fourth page when she saw the amount that was borrowed. It was the complete value of what the business was worth today and Edward had only given a third of the money when they started the business. Rose had to blink several times to fight back the heat of tears that threatened to fall.

"You know, I saw you with Rebecca last night and I thought maybe you knew. I know Rebecca does business with you, at least that's what Edward had hoped would happen."

Numb and bleeding at the same time, Rose fell back on being polite and pushing her feelings to the back so she could deal with her emotions in private.

"Rebecca wanted to offer me an opportunity," Rose said.

Jonathan sat back and sighed.

"Oh, doing more cleaning jobs," he said in a low voice.

"No, she wants me to head a new department in her expanding business."

Jonathan sat up. "That's great news!"

Rose looked up still reeling from hearing this

man tear down the scaffolding of her life and then providing proof.

"I told them no. I wouldn't be able to do that and keep the business. I told Rebecca that I wanted to keep the business for the girls because it was the last thing Edward, and I did together."

Jonathan ran his hand over his beard and shook his head.

"Running a business has to be hard. I would think you would want as much time as you could get with the girls. It just seems to me that if you were working for someone else, you would have your time to yourself."

Rose had heard other people say that there were times when there were just no words. She was sitting composed and calm in front of Jonathan, but a screaming squall was raging inside. Rose was always the responsible one. She was always the one who did the right thing and went the right way. Years of living a certain way didn't collapse when all of the other rules did.

"I wasn't thinking about me but the girls. I wanted to give them something from their father," Rose said in a calm voice.

"Was it a final no? Could you go back?" Jonathan prodded hopefully.

Rose heard the desperation in Jonathan's voice and thought about the number she had seen in the contract and then it all came together.

"You already know how much the business is worth, don't you?"

Jonathan had the grace to look away. "I've waited as long as I could. I tried to give you some time to settle after Edward's death. I thought he had told you. The other reason I came is because I think I have a buyer for the business."

"What?"

Jonathan ran his hands through his hair. "Listen, this was a hard decision. I have my own issues and I need the money. It's a bad deal, I get that, but you have an opportunity and so while it's bad timing, it might work best for us all."

Rose stood up and looked at Jonathan.

"I think it's time for you to go," Rose said.

"Really? You can't do this now. Edward never said you were one for drama. The buyer will be here today to go over numbers and how he would handle the transitions and what contracts would come with it."

"Well, you can tell your buyer he would get a business, but the contracts are mine. All of them are for me and not part of the company sale. So, you want a cleaning business, fine but that's all you'll get."

Jonathan grits his teeth. "That will reduce the value of the sale."

"Yes it will, won't it?" Rose turned and walked to her front door.

"Rose, think of this as a way to start over. I've looked at the books and seen the work you've been doing alone and the reputation you've created."

"Goodbye Jonathan. I'll get in contact with you as soon as I decide on the formalities."

"This could have been easier," Jonathan said as he walked out.

"You're right, it could have been, but Edward made sure that wouldn't happen for either of us."

Rose closed the door and then leaned against it

so it would hold her up. She didn't stop herself from sliding to the floor and she didn't try to wipe away the first hot fat tear that hit her hand. Instead, she lifted her left hand and looked at the almost faded circle where she used to wear her ring. The ring was gone. Edward was gone and soon everything else she had hoped to preserve for her girls would be gone.

She didn't fight it this time. Rose leaned her head back and let the tears come. When the deep gasps and intermittent moans joined in, she let herself wallow in the pain of disillusionment.

CHAPTER 6

*G*rayson wasn't sure how you asked a woman to be your fake fiancé but after the morning he had, he wasn't sure he could ask that of Rose. A man named Jonathan Castle called him to ask him to sign a contract with Rose's agency with him. Grayson thought him rude but when he said Rose was selling, he knew a lot of things but the woman he met last night wasn't interested in selling. Grayson wanted to meet Rose, but he wanted to help her if he could. He'd find the actress if he had to, but Patti had always said you take care of people first.

He thought about leaving her alone when he texted her and she said she wasn't feeling well but Grayson couldn't let it go. He had cajoled and begged her to come. He wasn't so sure this park meeting was the best idea when she suggested it but in light of current events, he thought it would make her feel better if she had the option to just leave.

Grayson walked into the park and walked past the Claw's house. He kept walking until he found the manmade duck pond. He used to come here with Patti and there was Rose sitting alone. He had been debating if he should call her and cancel. Looking at her alone and seeing how forlorn she was, he knew he had made the right decision.

Rose was sitting on a bench on the side of the pond. She was dressed in faded jeans and a purple vee neck shirt. Her hair was pulled back into a ponytail and she was looking out at the pond. He knew she was going through a rough time, but her shoulders were still squared back. The strength of character once again got him. Rose was no weeping willow. Grayson took a step towards her, and she turned to him with a tremulous smile.

"You found me," she said. Grayson shrugged.

"I told you everyone knew where you were," he said with a smile.

"I don't know if that is true, but I'll go with it today."

"Did you come ravenous for lobster," I asked.

"I don't know if I'm all that hungry after all and —"

"Hold before you come up with a woman excuse why eating at any time and everything is bad. I want you do know I am using food to loosen you up and get rid of that stress in your shoulders."

Rose smiled. "Oh, is that what food does?"

"Yes, it's so therapeutic. If we are really lucky, we'll eat something so delicious we'll feel obligated to sit on the bench and rub our tummies saying mmm, mmm good."

Rose reluctantly laughed and to Grayson it was one of the most welcome sounds of the day.

"I passed the claws place; do you want me to get some lobster rolls and a drink? It's the lunch special."

Grayson ran over to get the food and comes back with fours rolls.

"Grayson, who is this hungry?"

"If we aren't then maybe the rolls aren't what they say they are," Grayson said wiggling his eyebrows.

"Okay, let me say that from now on I'll get the food," Rose said as she took the roll. As they both begin to eat, Grayson decided it's time to start telling the truth.

"So, do you remember me telling you that I had been stood up?" he said.

"Yes, but really I thought that was just part of a line," Rose murmured, embarrassed.

"Nope, it wasn't. I was there because I had a problem and a woman I thought was going to fix it was supposed to meet me there."

He saw Rose stop chewing and then look at him sideways.

"You thought I was that woman?"

Grayson popped the last piece of the roll into his mouth as he nodded. He saw Rose finish half of her roll and then put it back in the container.

"If I remember correctly, you thought I was an actress," Rose said. "An actress? What was it about me that said actress?"

Grayson looked at her getting indignant and smiled. He would rather see this feisty Rose than the lost one he walked in on.

"It was the clothing and not caring what others would say. When you grow up in a small town you can become opinion sensitive."

Rose nodded.

"It's true, you can. I've been here for a couple of years. I'm a transplant, not a native Inheritance Bay gal. Do you dress to impress the town?" she asked.

Grayson smiled. "You think I dress to impress? Am I impressing you Rose Sallow?"

"Like I told you, I'm not a native. I've lived other places."

Grayson leaned forward. "Andddd?"

"And you rank high on the list."

"Wow, high on the list. With such a blow to my ego and after I brought food to you, I think I may need a second date to recover."

Rose laughed then. "A second date, huh?"

"Yes, I'd like to see you again."

"You are my employer."

"Ah yes, that. We need to talk about that. I'm an upfront kind of person."

Rose looked at his face. "I don't know if I could take any more truths for this day."

Grayson gathered the food on the far side of Rose.

"Why don't we swap and share. I think we can help each other," Grayson said.

"Okay, here goes nothing. I'm about to lose my business to an unexpected debt," Rose blurted out.

"I'm about to lose my home to an unfulfilled promise," Grayson said.

"What? That sounds crazier than mine," Rose said.

"It's true but the past has a way of catching up and haunting you," Grayson said.

Rose nodded. "That is so true."

"On a brighter note, your problem seems way more solvable," Grayson said.

Rose snorted. "It might if I had the money. Although, there is a whole lot more wrong than just the money, however money would help."

"Well, let me take that worry off of your shoulder. I'll give you the money," Grayson said.

Rose looked up at him wide-eyed and then laughed. Grayson hadn't expected that response.

"I'm not sure if I should be insulted or not," Grayson said.

Rose waved him off.

"Listen, let's just say you had the money. I couldn't take it. I wouldn't be able to say when I'd give it back. On top of that, not to be judgy but you don't look like you have the money to be giving out to me."

"Ouch!"

Rose patted his knee. "Look, I'm just trying to say thank you, but I wouldn't want to put you out. Besides I couldn't just take your money."

"Okay, do you have another option?"

"Well, I have one, but it won't save my business, but it will provide better income."

"Isn't that a good thing, having more money?" Grayson asked.

Rose slowly nodded. "I thought I was saving something special for my girls. Now I'm not so sure."

"Okay, despite that earlier disparaging remark on my funds, listen to my idea before you say anything."

Rose nodded.

"It turns out that my mother, Patti, always wanted me to marry and settle down. If I'm honest I always wanted to settle down with a great woman who liked simple things and wouldn't mind living in Inheritance Bay. I thought I had found her. I told my mom I was bringing her. Well, she broke up with me that night actually. So, in order to get the only home, I've ever known, I have to bring my fiancé here."

"Oh no! Patti didn't know," Rose said horrified. Grayson wished he could believe that but he his mom was one insightful woman.

"Well, be that as it may, I need a fiancé and despite my outer trappings I do make excellent money to be able to help you." He watched as it finally dawned on Rose what he was asking.

"Grayson are you asking me to be your fiancé?"

"For a short period of time, yes."

"And you'd give me the money to save my business?"

"I'd give you the money even if you said you didn't want to help me out, but I don't think you'd take it."

"You're right, I wouldn't. You do know your idea is madness and who would believe it? I mean I live here. Who would believe we were a thing? My husband passed just last year."

"Love at first sight? I know things are hard for you and if you are dealing with Jonathan Castle, that I imagine it must be a real pain."

He saw Rose stiffen. "You know Jonathan?"

Grayson could see her jumping to conclusions. The thoughts of betrayal and collusion were painted on her face. He reached out and grabbed her hand.

"I don't know Jonathan like that. He called me

yesterday asking if I would sign a contract with him. He told me the cleaning service was going to new ownership and it was a formality. I told him I'd get back to him. I don't plan on getting back to him, he was a pushy mess."

"Yeah, that's one way to say it."

"So, your thoughts?"

He could see Rose thinking about it.

"First, I don't think anyone would believe it."

"We'll say we were being discreet," Grayson said.

"It's crazy."

"It's an idea to help us both."

"I need time," Rose whispered.

Grayson was thrilled. She hadn't said no, and it looked like they would be able to help each other.

"I think you need ice cream."

"Ice cream?" Rose echoed confused.

"Yup, when I have big life decisions to make, I think it helps me when I have a big influx of sugar. In this case, the only sugar I see any hope of us having is ice cream!"

Rose sighed. "I guess so. I mean the fact that I've survived this day, I should probably get something as a reward."

"You go girl! It's about the now and making it work. Let's go make the ice cream guy do some work."

Grayson takes Rose to the ice cream cart and her eyes widen like a kid in a candy store. Again, he was amazed by her resilience. Today had to have been a horror for her. He knew she probably hadn't even really processed it all but still, she was here. It spoke volumes about her as a woman and a person. The problem was he was liking everything he was finding out about Rose Sallow and not just to help him with his fake fiancés problem.

They walk away with soft cones rolled in rainbow sprinkles. As Rose gets to the end of the cone she looked at him and smiled.

"Thanks. I didn't know it, but I needed this."

"You're welcome. What else can I do for you today?"

"I've got to go finish some invoices and review my choices. It seems like they are expanding in new ways," Rose said.

"I know its unorthodox, but I'd like you to think about it. If you say yes we can go over the details until you are comfortable. Also, remember if you don't want to do that the money is still yours Rose, no strings attached."

She huffed. "You know if you just go around offering to pay bills sight unseen on the amount for women, I can't imagine anyone standing you up for dinner."

Grayson leaned closer to her until their foreheads were touching.

"The beauty of it is you have to show up and put in the time first," Grayson said devilishly.

Rose stepped back and gave him a tremulous smile.

"I've got an appointment."

"No worries, I guess I can make it until tomorrow," Grayson said.

"Did I agree to lunch?"

"Lunch you say? I'm glad you brought it up. I'll text you."

Grayson saw her hesitate and wondered if he had pushed too hard.

"Fine, text me but it can't be anything special, I'll be working."

"Done!" He watched her walk away and for once the king of fundraising and making the deal wasn't sure if he was going to be able to close this one.

CHAPTER 7

Rose got into her car and let her head rest on the wheel. She had already been through the wringer and the day wasn't over. The girls would be out of school soon and that meant she only had a little time to get things done. Then her phone pinged.

I'M THINKING JAPANESE.

Rose looked at the text and laughed. Then she looked out of her window and saw Grayson texting. When their eyes met he turned as if he had been caught.

I HAVEN'T EVEN LEFT THE PARK.

I WANTED TO SECURE MY TIME. JAPANESE OKAY?

YES.

Then Rose looked to the side to see Grayson give a celebratory yell. He was the bright part of the day. When her phone rang she looked to see Grayson is gone, then she hears Portia.

"I want you to know that I have special skills and

53

powers that say you are holding out," Portia said.

"What are you talking about?"

"Well, I am working on a project with Gloria Danvers whose brother just opened the Claws house. She couldn't wait to ask me about you and Grayson in the park. I had to pretend it was hush-hush when in fact my bestie is meeting a man in public incognito. How can this not be holding out?"

Rose had to laugh. It was so hard to get used to small-town networks. The small-town network moved faster than a brush fire.

"Then let me give you the scoop. We are doing Japanese tomorrow."

"Two days in a row! He must be a paragon! So, you are really liking him."

"I'm finally doing what you suggested is all."

"I can hear the smile in your voice."

"Well, I'm taking myself home to do some work. When I've checked off some accomplishments for the day, I'll call you."

Rose hadn't been in her home for more than thirty minutes. The first thing she did when she got home was to take a shower. The park was nice, but she was wearing some of the ice cream on her shirt. It just wouldn't do to have to explain to the twins why Mommy had ice cream and they didn't. Just as she had finished pulling on fresh jeans and the T-shirt, she heard her phone.

"Hello?"

"Rose, you've got to come down here. I've been trying to call you." It was Traci. School wasn't out, so Traci would be at the office taking care of paperwork and mail.

"Traci calm down, what's the matter?"

"Some men are here and one of them is a man named Jonathan Castle. He said he's an owner and he's looking through our books."

"I'm on my way," Rose said as she dashed out of the door.

~

When Rose walked into the office, Jonathan was showing a gentleman out. She waited until the man was out the door before addressing Jonathan.

"What are you doing here?" Rose hissed.

"I'm leaving. Rose, this looked like it might take a minute. I'll pick up the girls for you." Once again Rose was so grateful for her friends.

"Thanks, Traci."

After Traci leaves, Rose turns on Jonathan.

"Now, tell me what are you doing here?"

"I told you earlier. I need my money. I found a buyer for the business, but they wanted to look at the books."

"You already have a buyer?" Rose looked at him with suspicion. When Jonathan looked away, she knew he'd been planning this for a while.

"It's not like I didn't tell you I wanted to sell. I didn't want to tell you that there was a firm offer until after the buyer looked at the books."

"How long have you been talking to this buyer? I mean, you just got here, and you just told me about this whole thing, but if you have a buyer, you must have been looking for a while."

"I started looking for a buyer about four months ago," Jonathan said sheepishly

Rose couldn't believe what she was hearing.

"Four months ago?" Rose echoed in disbelief. Four months ago, Jonathan had decided to change her life and the girl's live forever.

"While you've been here, I've had to make some serious life calls. I lost my job and I've only been able to get contract jobs here and there. I need this to work out and it needs to work out now."

Rose listened to Jonathan and realized she was done and over it. In the run of a day, all that she knew had changed or been shown not to be the truth. She was tired of trying to hold on to the broken dreams that could no longer be held up to the light.

Rose took a seat and looked at Jonathan.

"Okay, I give up. If you want to sell the business to save yourself, fine. I have options so I and the girls will be okay."

Jonathan took a seat nearby.

"It's not the way I wanted this to be. You don't know but when Edward first asked me for this money, he said it was only for a couple of months."

Rose looked at Jonathan incredulously.

"What did you think that Edward did that could give you that kind of money back in a couple of months?" Rose asked. Jonathan looked side to side and for a moment Rose thought he wasn't going to answer.

"Edward was good at gambling most of the time. I had seen him win that much money and more. It was only a matter of time before he did it again."

"Gambling?" Rose said in a whisper.

"Yeah, he was good." Jonathan praised.

"I didn't know," Rose whispered. Jonathan looked up at her shocked.

"I always wanted to know what he told you when he left for days at a time?"

Rose looked at Jonathan and shrugged. "He said he had a remote consulting job. Most of the time he went away he would come back with a decent bit of money to put towards the kids and the business."

Rose stood up not wanting to think about how she really didn't know Edward after all. Since Jonathan wanted to sell the business and the business was now a reminder of all the lies that were told to her and that she believed without question, it hurt but not quite as much to let it go.

"You know, Edward always said you wanted the two of you to spend more time with the girls. I know the business gave you little time together."

"It's true I didn't have as much time with the girls with the business. However, it was my choice how to allot my time. I didn't need you or Edward to take that decision from me."

Jonathan ran his hands through his hair and shrugged.

"Look it's done. The buyer liked the numbers, even if the business comes with no contracts. He thinks it still a solid business."

"I'm glad someone sees the value in it," Rose murmured. "When is the sale date?" Rose choked out the question.

"I'm trying to move it as soon as possible. I think we will both be happier."

Rose rubbed her forearms and looked around the office. It held so many memories. She would have to move all of the furniture and equipment somewhere.

"Did you sell the furniture with the company?"

"Yes," he murmured. Rose nodded. It seemed like nothing would be left. She had options. She picked up an item or two and walked toward the door. This phase of her life was over. It would take some time for her to accept it, but she had options. She was going to embrace her new life and be the best mother she could be to her girls. It also looked like she was about to become a fiancé. She didn't need the money to buy the business, but Rebecca's job didn't start until November or December. She would need some funds to take care of her and the girls. It would also give her time to make sure the girls started school off right.

It wasn't the way she wanted but she was about to get a new lease on life. She needed to make one call. Rose waited until she was home, and Traci said she was on the way before she called Grayson.

"Grayson?"

"Yes."

"Are you still looking for a fiancé?"

"No, I'm waiting for you to say yes."

Rose smiled. Grayson was the only consistent thing in the whole day.

"Well, then let me put you out of your misery. Yes, Yes I will be your fiancé."

"Lunch should be exciting then."

Just then Traci opened the door, and the twins came pouring into the house.

"Mom! Mom! Look what we did —"

"Those are your kids," Grayson said but he was cut off when the girls came closer, and Rose couldn't hear what Grayson was saying.

"I've got to go and yes those are my girls. We'll talk tomorrow."

CHAPTER 8

*G*rayson tossed and turned all night. Rose's girls sounded so small and animated. He couldn't recall why but he thought they were older. They were so young and in that moment Grayson's plan fell apart. He was going to have to tell Rose that he'd give her the money, but he'd find someone else to be his fiancé.

Grayson had picked up the phone several times this morning to text her that there will be no lunch. Every time he got ready to call, he could see her radiant, strong smile. He could see her standing tall even though things were falling apart. He couldn't even remember the last time a woman had intrigued him. The problem wasn't Rose. Grayson was great around teenagers and young adults, but young children were so vulnerable. They formed attachments too quickly. Before he was adopted he had met a lot of "uncles" who didn't stay around. Each one made him feel as though he had done something to send them away. Patti had always told him otherwise but when you're a young kid, you knew it all. As a result, he didn't date or hang around women with young kids and Grayson was pretty sure the little girls he heard were young.

While Grayson was trying to find the words to break it off with Rose, a text comes in. THIS IS WHAT YOUR FIANCÉ DOES WHEN SHE'S NOT WITH YOU. The picture that came with the text was of Rose and two identical copies of her. All of them were sitting down at a little table having tea. One girl had her hair in two ponytails and the other girl had one ponytail. All of them were laughing at something at the table.

His resolve was firm he couldn't do this. He wouldn't be his father, a person who walked in and out of a young child's life scarring them and making them doubt their own self-worth. Just looking at the picture brought back memories of his own childhood. He was so desperate for love and affection that he would always try to be the quiet child. It didn't make a difference how quiet he was. It didn't make a difference how well he listened. Eventually, all of the uncles went away, and Grayson was left thinking there was something wrong with him.

He still wanted to help. He would just have to do it from afar. An idea started to form in his head.

WHERE DO I SEND THE MONEY?

WE'LL TALK AT LUNCH.

BEST TO TAKE CARE OF THIS FIRST.

Grayson waits for her to text the information and instead his phone goes off. He practically dropped it. He brought the phone to his forehead and wondered what he was going to do. What he needed were his brothers. Reid would be here soon enough, but it wasn't helping him now.

WHAT'S WRONG?

Grayson never thought of himself as a coward but right now he had to admit it wasn't one of his finer moments.

NOTHING IS WRONG. YOU'RE PERECT.

WOW IT'S THAT BAD! WE'LL TALK LATER.

He smiled. Rose was smarter than most and just what he thought he needed. He rolled the idea in his head all morning. He didn't think he could do it. He couldn't risk influencing a child's life. He didn't have any kids and wasn't sure how he would even address a child.

The day flew by, and lunch was almost upon him. He still wasn't any closer to finding a solution to the problem. He needed to give the money to Rose but tell her the fiancé thing was off.

ARE YOU READY TO TALK TO ME?

Grayson looked at the text and smiled. That was Rose. She was tenacious. It would normally be one of the things he admired but now it was in his way. Grayson went over his list again. Rose was attractive inside and out. She was easy going, had an amazing work ethic and faithful. No matter how many great qualities she may have, Grayson was firm in his mind that the children always came first. He wouldn't be a part of that cycle of hurting a child, even if it was unintentional.

I WAS WRONG TO ASK.

AH, YOUR ACTRESS CAME THROUGH.

NO

THEN IT'S ME. THAT'S OKAY

IT'S NOT YOU. IT'S ME.

Grayson was waiting for her to respond and when it didn't come he felt lower than a snake's belly. He was going over how he had messed this up. Then the phone rang, and he grabbed it.

"Hello Mr. Chance, this is Jonathan Castle."

Grayson wanted to hang up but manners and a long career in fundraising that gave him the tolerance he needed right now.

"I know you Mr. Castle. I haven't changed my mind about signing the contracts. How can I help you?"

"I wanted to know if I could talk to you. There have been some new changes that you should be aware of. Just five minutes of your life please."

By the time the call was over, Grayson had agreed to speak to Jonathan. The good news, if there was good news, was that it was over. He was disappointed that the call hadn't been from Rose, but it was probably for the best. Grayson tried to think what he would tell Mr. Dane. He could try appealing to the new owners or buy the house when it goes up on market. He looked up at the clock, it was an hour before he was supposed to meet Rose. Grayson brought his thoughts back to the task at home. He tried to throw himself into work. He had several charities that had asked him to raise funds for them. He was kicking around some ideas in his head when he heard the knock on the door.

Standing at the door was Rose. She's amazing. Her hair is in a sloppy ponytail. She's had on a white frilly top and dark black jeans that accentuated her lean legs. In her hand, she had a bag from the Japanese place where they were supposed to go to.

"You've got to know the "it's me not you" is not an answer. It seemed like you were having a problem talking which is so out of character, so I brought lunch so we could discuss it. If you've changed your mind about the fiancé thing, I get it. Just tell me, Grayson. If I'm just not the one for you, you can say that."

Grayson steps back so she can come in.

"I didn't handle this well. I'm glad you came by. I want to make sure you get the money to save your business."

"I'm not taking charity. If you don't want to do the plan, I'm good but —"

"But it is me," Grayson said as he takes the food and walks them to his kitchen.

"Grayson talk to me," Rose said.

Grayson turns to tell her. He owed her that much.

"The problem is -" Then the bell rang. Grayson can't believe it. He'd been in Inheritance Bay in the rental for a couple of weeks and no one had come to see him. Right when he needed to tell Rose something important, now he gets guests. Frustrated he opens the door.

Jonathan Castle is standing with a tentative smile on his face.

"Mr. Chance." Grayson looked at him and thinks this is all his fault. He wouldn't be trying to help the best woman he had ever met if this man didn't want money. It was all so senseless. Maybe his brother Reid was right, that money changes everything and almost always for the worst. This man thinks he's getting the upper hand on Rose. Hitting him isn't a realistic option. Then Grayson looked over his shoulder and sees Rose looking on confused and unsure. Then time stops and Grayson just goes with the moment like he's done so many other times.

"Jonathan, have you met my fiancé?" Grayson said holding out his hand to Rose, hoping she'll take it.

Rose puts on a wide smile and waves at Jonathan.

"Jonathan and I have already met. Although, I have to say, I'm so much happier meeting you under these better circumstances."

"Oh, is this the Jonathan that you were talking about who wanted to go ahead and sell the company?"

Jonathan is standing at the door, shifting from one foot to the other. Grayson is totally engrossed in looking at Rose.

"Ah well, I've already spoken to Rose. It's my understanding that she has agreed to sell and so this transaction has no bad feelings amongst any of us," Jonathan said.

"You must have fallen on hard times to have to sell the company," Grayson said.

"Well, the cleaning business isn't what I'd call a great long-term investment," Jonathan said in response.

"I'm surprised you want to be bothered getting a buyer for it then. I mean since it's not really high on money makers and all," Rose said sweetly.

"Well, it's all about striking when you have a buyer. You know it has a lot to do with why and how people choose investments. You want to do it when opportunities come," Jonathan said. Grayson saw where this was going and decided to intervene, otherwise he was going to have to step in.

"Jonathan, I'm sure you came here for a reason," Grayson said.

"Well, yes, it was like I said on the phone. I wanted to make sure that you knew that the company was being sold and that your contract would be welcomed," Jonathan said with a glint in his eye.

"I'm not able to make a decision right now, but even when I do make one, that decision will be handled by my fiancé," Grayson said as he put his arm around Rose.

"Well then, there should be no problem at all, should there Rose?" Jonathan asked.

"This isn't a good time for me to discuss this." Rose said as she blinked her eyes. Grayson had never seen her blink her eyes so much since he met her.

"Did you want to go over these things at dinner tonight?" Jonathan offered.

Grayson clears his throat.

"I'm sorry Jonathan, tonight isn't going to work, we have plans," Grayson said.

"Plans?" Jonathan echoed.

"Yes, she's busy with me."

"You two will have each other forever, it seems like business should get a first seat," Jonathan joked.

"Spoken like a man who's not totally besotted by the woman in his life. Maybe it's honeymoon syndrome but I can assure you with a woman like Rose, it's always about what she wants to do first."

With pursed lips, Jonathan gives a curt nod.

"Well, it seems like you two should do just fine together." With that, Jonathan nodded and left.

Grayson could tell Jonathan wanted to say so much more. He was feeling bad about it but then he looked over at Rose and she had a smile that could barely be contained.

"I know it's not nice or polite to be so happy that something finally stopped Jonathan's pushiness but a little part of me enjoyed that," Rose said.

"Let's eat the lunch you brought, and you can bring me up to speed," Grayson said. Grayson and Rose set up in the kitchen. She had taken one bite before she put her fork down and then turned to him.

"I'm sorry for the way that I acted when Jonathan was here. It seems as though there were a lot of things that I didn't know about my deceased husband. Edward took a loan out on the business from Jonathan. The loan would be value of the business today. Jonathan on the othe hand, seemed to have been his partner in crime. I was angry that I didn't know about the loan and to be honest, I've really just felt left out and hurt."

Grayson put his fork down mid-way to his mouth.

"I can see how you are in a unique position Rose. You are also one of the most levelheaded people that I've met in town recently, so there was no doubt in my mind that whatever you were willing to dish out to Jonathan he deserved."

"Well, if I'm the paragon of stability, maybe you can tell me why you were trying to break up with such a great fiancé?" she asked.

Grayson looked at an expectant Rose and sighed in frustration.

"The issue is your children," he said glumly.

"The twins? You don't like kids?"

"No, no it's not that. I actually do like kids. Well, I like when other people have kids. So, the thing is this. I don't want to get involved in their life or make them think that men come and go. I just —"

"Hold on. Let's take this one step at a time. You're worried about my girls getting attached to you?" Rose asked.

"Yes! That's it exactly. It's the worst when you think someone is going to be there and then they are poof! Gone."

Rose's hands covered her mouth.

"Grayson, that is the sweetest thing I've ever heard."

"What?"

"I just think it's so considerate and kind of you to think of my babies."

Grayson can see this is not having the effect he thought it would. Waving her hands in front of her eyes, Rose takes a big breath and reaches across to place her hand atop of Grayson's.

"Listen, my girls are five but quick as a whip. I do have friends that are guys, so you don't have to worry about that. As for their attachment, the girls and I talk all the time about if I will ever find them another daddy. I told them it doesn't just happen, and they agreed. It's also something we talk about, so you don't have to worry about that. I can understand your concern, but my girls are pretty good at just being friends with people."

Grayson listened to Rose, and it all sounded right. In fact, it sounded too good to be true.

"Let me also add in this little caveat. I like you. I

think you are a great guy but if we don't have this agreement, then I will not be taking your money."

Grayson groans. "So, we do this fake engagement. Do some show and tells for Mr. Dane, the attorney. He said he needs to meet with us both for me to get the deed and then we can see each other for a couple more times and then decide it's not for us."

Rose nods and then the both of them finish eating lunch.

"I'm glad I came over. As for the money, we can settle it when the sale of the business happens. I'm in no hurry and I'll make sure to tell my girls you are not interviewing for the daddy spot."

"I'm not but why don't we limit the interaction as much as possible? I'll feel better and I know you said you talked to the girls but just in case."

"Wow, you think you're that irresistible to the female sex."

Grayson smiled.

"I don't know if you've heard but I'm a Chance brother. We are all great catches.

CHAPTER 9

*R*ose left Grayson's house and started thinking about her to-do list. She had to call Rebecca and confirm the job. She had to talk with the girls about Grayson not being a daddy candidate, which was beyond sweet every time she thought about how concerned Grayson was. She was also going to have to call Traci about watching the twins while she was doing this fake fiancé thing. Finally, Rose knew she had to bring Portia up to speed as much as she could. This wasn't just about her. After Rose got in the door she called Portia to come to get her suit that started it all.

"Thanks for coming by Portia."

"How could I not come by? It seems this is the only way I'm going to get any details about the mystery man."

"It's no mystery. Grayson Chance is known by everybody in town."

"Yes, but he was fresh meat on the market."

"Fresh meat?"

Portia waved her hand and then took a seat on the living room couch.

"This is Inheritance Bay. It's true there are some new businesses coming in and things are looking up. You don't forget the people who grew up here. You certainly don't forget the guys who made an impression. The Chance brothers are the American story. All of them came to Patti Chance's foster home. Then all of them leave the nest and become successful businesspeople. It doesn't get more fairy tale than that."

"Well, it was almost a no-go."

"What? Is he some kind of snob? If he is, you don't have to take that, and I'll go talk to him myself."

Rose smiled. Portia was the best of friends. She was a little easy to get riled up, but you always knew she was on your side.

"No, it turns out that he was just concerned that I had children."

"He doesn't like children?"

"No, he was concerned that the babies would get attached to him."

Portia screamed.

"That is so hot in a guy today. It shows he's in touch with his feminine side."

Rose rolled her eyes.

"I don't know about him being in touch with his feminine side, but I will be seeing him."

"Well, that sounds promising. When are you going out next?"

Rose wasn't sure exactly when they were going out next. When she heard the text on her phone.

DO YOU WANT TO PICK DINNER?

I THOUGHT THAT WAS JUST FOR JONATHAN.

YOU STILL EAT DINNER DON'T YOU?

Rose smiled and shook her head.

"Are you giggling while you're texting? Oh, this is getting serious," Portia said as she wiggled her eyebrows.

"I'm not giggling," Rose protested.

I BROUGHT LUNCH. YOU PICK.

Rose put her phone away only to see Portia smiling at her as if she was the kitten who had just eaten the canary.

"I'm not saying anything either way. I think it's great you're getting out there and if you are going to take a chance, there is nothing wrong with taking it with a man who is gorgeous, smart, and can afford some of life's extras."

"I've got work to do and since I'm going out tonight, Traci is stopping by."

"I could have stayed with the twins," Portia said and again Rose thought she heard a little bit of longing in her voice that no one is allowed to speak about.

"Sophia wanted to see the twins. The girls haven't spent as much time with each other since Sophia has been going to her classes for her dyslexia."

"Of course."

There it was. That awkward silence that happened whenever children were brought up around Portia.

"Well, I'm going to be on my way, and let me know how the date goes," Portia said with her usual perky self as she went to the door.

"Hey, I just want you to know you're the best friend ever," Rose said.

"Thanks. You're not too bad yourself." Rose watched as Portia got into her car and she couldn't help but think that there was just something lurking under the surface that Portia needed to talk about. Ten minutes later, she got a text from Portia.

REMEMBER TO ASK IF HE HAS A FREE BROTHER!

Rose decided to make some chocolate chip cookies and cupcakes. She hoped these were still good desserts for Sophia. It seems like the kids grow up so fast. One day they like Jell-O and the next it's too kiddie and now they like cookies like the big kids. A couple of hours later, Rose heard the jingle in the door and then the stampede of feet, followed by the scream of cookies.

When she left her office, Rose sees Traci trying to fend off the children from the sweets. Then, as if they can smell the weaker one has entered the room, the kids turn to Rose and run smiling to her.

"Be strong!" Traci calls out with a laugh.

"Can we have a cookie and a cupcake, please?" Anna and Hannah her adorable twins ask, and Rose knows she's going to say yes.

"Okay, but only one!"

Traci comes over and gives Rose a hug. "How is that being strong?"

"I said only one," Rose countered. "Thank you for coming over on such short notice."

"You know I'm here to support you, especially if it's going out with a Chance brother," Traci said with a smile.

"Wow, does everyone know?"

Traci looked to the side as she tapped her finger on her forearm.

"No, I'm sure everyone doesn't know. I mean old lady Mildred can't hear much anymore so I'm sure she hasn't heard," Traci said with a smile. "You know how it is in small towns and returning heroes, and the Chance brothers would all count as returning heroes. Now stop worrying about what people are or aren't saying. Get ready to go out."

"About that, this may be a regular thing. I know you're busy with Sophia, so maybe I should make some other —"

"Don't even think it. We're always here for each other and I'm so happy for you in light of everything that is going on that you're able to move forward."

Rose pulled Traci into a hug and murmured thank you. Rose was feeling so conflicted about her not telling her friends everything. Her friends are supporting her but she's not telling them the complete truth. Rose can't help but make comparisons between what she's doing now and Edward. She just hopes her friends understand.

Rose knows it's a pet peeve, but he's late. Children are not very forgiving when it comes to time. Oh, it's true that they can be late, but parents very rarely can. A sporty black BMW pulls up in front of her house.

"Do you think people will notice us?" Grayson asked.

"They would have noticed us without the car. Now that we're in it everyone will have an excuse to say they saw us." Grayson got out of the car and held the door open for her. He was wearing a light blue shirt and dark blue slacks.

"You look beautiful by the way," he said in Rose's ear as she got into the car. Rose was glad that she had chosen to wear the blue dress with a crisscross sleeveless top and a skirt that fell just below her knees. As Grayson went to the driver's side, Rose was trying to calm her beating heart. This is just an act she said. Grayson is a great guy and he's just doing what he would for any woman. Rose hoped if she kept saying that mantra to herself that she would start to believe it and her head would take the lead from her feelings.

"I thought we'd go to an Italian place if you don't mind?" Grayson said.

"You're driving. It's your call."

"Great! I actually picked the place because I wanted someplace the whole town doesn't hang out, so we can get to know each other."

And just like that, with just a couple of words, all of a sudden it all became so very real for Rose. They were going to get to know one another?

"What would you like to know exactly?" Rose asked.

"It's not going to be an inquisition, just some basic things couples know about each other."

"I might not be the best person to tell you what couples know about each other. Especially in light of what I've learned about my Edward, I feel like some days I didn't know him at all."

"I can understand that. I told you before, I was engaged to be married. I thought Sheila and I were on the same page, but then, when I told her we were going to come back here to live, everything changed."

"Okay. So where would you like to start?"

"Have you accepted the job yet?"

"Not yet. It seems like getting in contact with Rebecca is a lot harder than it was before. I know that they are really putting a lot of effort into doing the expansion."

"Are you an only child?"

Rose sighed. She knew this was probably going to come up in conversation, but she never really liked talking about her family.

"I'm the oldest. My younger sister is named Lucy and I think she still lives in the city with my mother."

"Still lives in the city? You all don't live together?"

"No. When my parents divorced, each one of them decided to take a child. My mother didn't want to be alone, so she took Lucy. Probably she took Lucy because I didn't want to leave my dad."

"Wow, that's pretty rough. To have to choose between your parents, I mean. Do you ever go see your mother?"

"No, I don't go looking for them at all. The only time that my mother comes looking for me is when she needs something."

"I'm sorry."

"Some things you just have to accept as is. I think when I was younger I used to hope that one day my mom and my sister would just show up at the front door. That magic day of reconciliation never happened and I think my dad was hoping that it would happen, as well, but it didn't." Rose tried not to look at the past. She had accepted her mother leaving but she had never understood it. She hadn't told Grayson that her dad wasn't the same after her mother left, either.

"Unfortunately, I don't have that much better luck when it comes to mothers, either," Grayson said. "I wondered for a very long time why my birth mother didn't keep me. Finally, I caught up to her and asked her."

Rose turned to see him as he drove. She had never been brave enough to ask her mother why she chose Lucy. Rose always wanted to know, but she could just never bring herself to ask the question.

"And?"

"She told me she was young. She told me that when she first had me she thought it was going to change her life for the better. Instead, her family didn't give her any support. My father didn't stick around and after doing what she could, she gave me up."

The car stopped and Rose realized they had made to the restaurant. However, she had one question she had to ask.

"Was it enough? Did knowing make it better for you?"

Grayson looked over at Rose and gave her a sad smile.

"When I was a kid, I raged at everyone for her not being there. I swore I'd never forgive her. Then one day I met Patti and that was the beginning of me being so grateful to my birth mother. Patti was the angel who saved me, raised me and gave me all the love I could have ever wanted. So, knowing didn't make it better but it helped me to close that chapter and move on with my life. Speaking of moving on let's get inside and help some seafood move on to the next plane," Grayson said.

Rose laughed and realized Grayson Chance is the kind of man any woman would want to hold on to, maybe even her.

CHAPTER 10

Grayson had never told anyone the whole story about his mother or Patti. There was something about Rose that made everything easier to talk about. He had planned on them talking about their lives. After all, they had to go in front of Mr. Dane, and they wanted to make sure they looked credible. Grayson thought they would be exchanging information about their favorite color and their favorite food.

As she got out of the car, he couldn't help but notice the fresh smell of chocolate chip cookies. It was a reminder to him why he can't have anything between them. When they walked into the restaurant, it wass dimly lit, and he could tell there aren't a lot of patrons in tonight. All of the reasons he chose this place were turning out to be true.

Grayson had been here before, so he didn't wait for anyone to come to see them. He knew exactly where his table is.

"So, I want to tell you that every time I come here, I always order the special," Grayson said.

"The special? What is it?"

"Well, it changes every time but most of the time it's some kind of pasta and seafood."

Rose nodded and gave him a wan smile.

"I feel like you're telling me this for a reason."

"I'm saying that while we're getting to know each other maybe we should live a little."

"Ah, you don't want to be alone in this adventure," she said with a knowing smile. "No problem, I will add that to your list of attributes. He likes to try new things."

Grayson looked over at Rose and realized she's smiling at him.

"Okay, what's the smile about?"

"I see. I'm going to have to be very careful with you, Grayson. You really are used to getting just about everything you want."

Grayson tried to look appalled.

"It's not about me getting what I want. It's about us doing the best thing." The both of them laughed after his ridiculous statement. Again, there it was creeping up on him like a shadow and fitting him like a glove. It just felt right to be with Rose.

"Grayson! Today must be a blue moon on a leap day, you are here with someone and it's a woman, not a business partner," Carlo exclaims. Then Carlo turned his attention to Rose.

"Ah lady, you must be something special besides the obvious beauty that I see. If I was just fifteen years younger and not already married forty-five years to my soul mate, Isabella, I'd take you right away from Grayson."

Grayson watched as Rose blushed under the compliment and Grayson had to remember that Carlo wasn't competition, just a harmless flirt.

"If only you could get our food as quickly as you're able to drop those compliments."

Carlo turned to face Grayson.

"She must indeed be a special woman if she has the ability to make you feel jealous."

Grayson was going to deny it but realized that would only get him in deeper water.

"I see I've teased Grayson enough. Young lady, Grayson helped us get this restaurant. When my Isabella and I only had recipes from the old country, Grayson helped us find funding for this place. He's a good boy."

Rose smiled at him, and Grayson felt like he was sitting on the highest mountain.

"It seems this is the night to learn all sorts of things about Grayson," Rose said.

"The other thing that I really like about Grayson is that he is so consistent. I bet you tonight, he wants to order the special?"

Grayson met Rose's gaze across the table, and he could see she was doing all she could not to laugh.

"I think you have a great idea, Carlo. I hear your specials are all the rave," Rose said.

Not even thirty minutes later a penne pasta with seafood came out. They were about halfway through when Rose picked up her phone. Grayson saw her texting but knew it was serious when she started to nibble on her bottom lip.

Grayson caught Carlo's eye and Carlo came right away.

"The food was excellent as always, but I think we

are going to be leaving soon," Grayson said looking at Rose.

"Yes, I'm sorry but Anna isn't well. It's probably my fault."

Carlo took the meals to pack them, and Grayson reached over and placed his hand on Rose's.

"What's your fault?"

"Anna's probably sick because she ate too many chocolate chip cookies. I should have been firmer with the girls and told them no."

"This is going to be fine. If a stomachache was the end of the world, I would have never made it out of childhood. Besides, I don't mind. I can stay a bit just in case they need anything."

Rose stopped and looked at him confused.

"You give me mixed signals Grayson," she murmured.

"It's not a mixed message, Rose. I just don't want it to be that as soon as you get home to take care of your girls and they need something and then you have to run back out again. I'll stay in the car and wait a little while and then if you don't need anything I'll just go home."

"Anna has an upset stomach, not Ebola Grayson. You can come into the house. Besides, I have to introduce you as a friend some time andit'ss always easier to introduce people to the girls one at a time."

Grayson wanted to say no, let's wait until like never but instead he smiled and nodded. Saying hello to a child and saying you're going to be a part of their life isn't the same thing, but Grayson looked at Rose and she seems so sure. He's going to trust her and do this. Besides, it's one meet and greet and if it goes the wrong way he'll leave.

"Okay, let's meet the twins," Grayson said.

~

Rose didn't seem concerned in the restaurant but as he was driving her home he heard her fingers flying over her phone and the dings going back and forth are like a musical recital.

"I'm sorry that this has happened," Rose said. "Anna's keeping the seltzer down so she should be fine."

"I was thinking we'd try to do another get-together before we saw Mr. Dane. At this point, we're just like most couples in the United States. The man knows nothing, and the woman knows all there is to know about the guy."

Rose lifted her head up and then just laughed.

"Okay you managed to get my attention, that is definitely worth another shot at getting through dinner." Grayson glanced over to see that Rose was still nervous.

"Any tips you want to give me on how to deal with Hannah?"

"Actually, out of the two of them, Hannah is theeasier-goingg twin."

"They're five," Grayson said with a smile.

"You never know how kids are going to take things or interpret them. Anna was watching a television show. Nothing racy, it was a television show about a family living in early history. Well, after Anna became very clingy and wouldn't let me go into a room by myself and she didn't want me to go into a room with another adult, either. Finally, we talked about it, and she was acting so strange because she said every time an adult went into a room on the television show another child showed up. She didn't want a brother or sister, so she thought she was saving me."

Grayson heard the story and laughed.

"Okay, you've got me there. I would have never put that one together."

"Welcome to children."

"Do you know when the new job will start?" he asked.

"No, but I'm hoping after the twin's birthday."

"When is that?"

"It's in three weeks. Three weeks to find the perfect gift for both of them. Which is like no time at all," Rose moaned.

"They're five years old, how hard can it be?"

Rose laughed. "Spoken like an innocent. Just because they are younger doesn't mean they don't have personality and quirks. In fact, I sometimes think they go out of their way to be different sometimes and it creates more challenges."

"I guess I never thought about those sweet little girls being a problem."

"I tell my girlfriend, Portia, who can't believe the girls are anything but perfect to imagine twenty years added to them and then tell me what you see?"

"By the way, I have a meeting with Mr. Dane. I'm going to ask him if he wants me to bring my fiancé and that way we can move this along. I know you want to get on with your new job and I want to move my stuff in, as well."

"When do you think you're going to be moving in?"

"I was hoping to move in no later than October, but we'll see."

"Are you a big Halloween fan?"

Grayson smiled. "As a matter of fact, I think that Halloween is the best holiday of them all. Don't your girls like Halloween?"

"They love Halloween. It's the preparation and then the going through the candy and then the subsequent tummy aches later that I don't like about Halloween."

Grayson had started talking so that he could calm down Rose. However, as they were getting closer to the house, he found that he was the one who was feeling a little unsettled. He was just going to meet a little girl. How hard could that be? At the same time, he was thinking this, his stomach was starting to cramp. Grayson couldn't believe he was more nervous going to see the five-year-old than he had been to meet up with Rose. He just had to keep his head straight. She was a little girl, and this would be over before he knew it.

When they arrived at Rose's house. He took the time to open her door and calm down. Rose scrambled out of the car and immediately went for her front door. Grayson felt as though he was walking to his doom. What was he doing here? He knew what the rules were, and he had reason for these rules.

It's a one-time event and Rose said she's already taken care of explaining him. He just needed to remind himself. Hannah is only five years old. She probably won't want to talk to him at all because he's an adult.

A woman throws the door open, and Grayson

can only assume that it's Traci her friend. He looked around the room, trying to see if the five-year-old is anywhere in sight. With any luck, she'd be in bed. As Grayson is looking for the elusive Hannah, he sees that the house is welcoming and comfortable. The furniture seems to be oversized but made for sitting. In the air, he could smell traces of cookies and cupcakes.

In fact, if he were honest, he was surprised that the only hint that there were twin girls in the house was a small table that was set up for tea. At the table were two dolls and there were four settings at the table. As an afterthought as Rose and the other woman were going down the hall, Rose turned around and looked at him.

"Anna is in the back. I'll be back out as soon as I can."

Grayson took a seat on the comfy couch and waited. Waiting on a couch, wasn't something that he found himself doing very often. Then Grayson heard the little scratching noise. He had been in foster homes where there were mice, so he knew right away it wasn't a mouse.

"Are you my mother's friend?" A young firm voice asked from behind the couch.

Grayson did his best not to smile. He knows this is a serious question and a serious moment. However, he didn't expect to get a third degree from a five-year-old who was behind the couch.

"I am your mother's friend. And you are?"

Then a little girl popped up in front of him with blonde pigtails dressed in a hot pink leotard.

"You don't know who I am?"

Grayson could hear the slight tone of indignation in her voice.

"Well, I can't say that I've ever met you."

"If you talk to my mother at all, then you'd know who I am."

"Your mother did say she was going to introduce us tonight."

"You said you'd meet a stranger?"

"Well, you're not really a stranger if your mom knows you."

The girl looked at him as if she was trying to size him up. For a moment, Grayson was worried that he might not come up to snuff. Then, as if she had figured it all out, she let out a small breath, and then she held her hand out.

"I'm Hannah. What's your name?"

"My name is Grayson."

"Grayson? I think I saw a show where one of the wolves were named Grayson. Can you turn into a wolf?"

"No, I can't," Grayson said trying to keep a straight face.

"Well, it's okay. I'm sure one day you'll find out how to do something."

She patted him on his hand, and he could see her brown eyes were just like her mother's, full of empathetic emotion and heartfelt sympathy.

"Auntie Traci said that you can be whatever it is that you really put your mind to. So maybe if you think about it really hard, one day you can be a wolf, too."

"Do you know what you're going to be when you grow up?"

"I am going to be a ballerina."

"Ah, you like to dance?"

Hannah gave him a disappointed look.

"No, but I love wearing my pink leotard and my mom said that I am so cute. That people love looking at me. So, I'm going to keep my leotard on all the time and travel around with the dancing company."

"So, are you and your sister going to have the same job?"

"No, and she doesn't like to dress up in my clothes."

"What does she like to do?"

"She likes animals. So, she's going to grow up and be an animal doctor."

"So, you won't have to dance? Are you sure?"

Totally exasperated with him she shakes her head.

"It's okay if you don't know that. My mom said that lots of people don't know things."

Grayson tries to make sure that he's not laughing.

"Well, it was nice to meet you."

And just like that, Grayson felt as though he's been dismissed. Just as Hannah is leaving, Rose came into the room.

"Is everything okay in here?" Rose asked.

Before Grayson can get a word in edgewise, Hannah answered the question.

"I'm fine, thank you. I met Grayson and he doesn't seem like a bad person."

"Thank you very much, Hannah," Grayson said graciously. When Hannah turns around and faces Grayson, her face looked curious and there is a gleam in her eye that tells Grayson he needs to prepare himself.

"Can you read stories?"

"Yes, I can read stories," Grayson confirmed. Then Hannah turns to her mom and gifts her with a big smile.

"Since Anna is sick. Can he read me my bedtime story?"

"Hannah, you just met him and maybe he doesn't want to read you a bedtime story."

Hannah was completely confused. Then she turned back and faced Grayson.

"You can read, right? I mean, you can read big people's stories. Like second-grade books?"

Grayson can't even articulate a word without laughing. He just nods his head. Hannah turned back around in order to face her mom.

"I can read books, but I think we should listen to your mother and maybe I'll read to you another time?" Grayson said trying to back out gently. Hannah gave him a long look and then nodded.

"You know my mom said when you are going to do something, do your best. You can practice and then you can read to me when you feel better."

With that, she leaves, and Grayson feels a sense of foreboding. What was he doing? Did he just promise a child he'd be back to read a story to her? He needed to leave.

"Hey Grayson, I'm sorry about tonight. I'll make it up to you. I wanted to say thank you."

Grayson saw Rose taking a step toward him and he knew where this was going. In fact, not even ten minutes ago, he would have thought that this night would have ended with a goodnight kiss in her living room. All of those thoughts had been there before he met Hannah. Now he wasn't sure what he was thinking. Then Grayson did something that shocked them both. When Rose was close enough he picked up her hand, turned it over, and kissed her wrist.

"Good night Rose. It's been a pleasure."

He saw the surprise on her face, but he didn't answer it or let it stop him. He left Rose and drove to the front of the foster home. It was ridiculous to want to live in this house. He was a single man without a family and this house was made for children and a family. When he thought about all of the good times that he had there with his brothers, suddenly it didn't seem so crazy. He wasn't sure how he was going to make it happen, but he was going to go back home.

The real problem here is that now when he thought about home. He thought about a little girl in the pink leotard. Maybe he was wrong. Maybe it was never about the children getting attached to him. Maybe it was about Grayson getting attached to them. Grayson wasn't ready to face those thoughts and all that they would entail.

CHAPTER 11

*P*ortia came by the next morning bearing croissants and scones.

"Wow, you must want information pretty badly to come bearing these types of gifts," Rose said.

Portia smiled. "Listen, I'm not saying I'm here for anything, but as your friend, I'm here if you want to share. I want you to know that I'm here for you, and my ears are open and listening, for you, that is."

"Anna was sick last night, and he brought me home early. Then when I thought he was going to kiss me, he picked up my hand and kissed me on my wrist," Rose said.

"So, what is that about?"

"I don't know. I know he's very concerned about my kids becoming dependent on him, or emotionally dependent is probably the better word. Hannah met him, and she thought she found a new story reader."

"That girl is a piston."

"Well, I don't know if Grayson thought the same thing," Rose said.

"How could he not? I mean, Hannah is gorgeous, bold, and so focused."

"I agree the twins are great, but I think asking him to read to her was too much like commitment."

"Well, did he say he'd do it?"

"No, Hannah gave him time to practice."

"That is so rich. I wonder if he knows the twins think later means tomorrow?"

"I don't know, but I think the whole reading a story idea was way more impactful to him than it was to Hannah." Rose wanted to go over how she could see the change in Grayson, but her phone rang, and it was Rebecca.

"Hey, Rebecca, can I see you today?"

"You sure can, especially if it's good news," Rebecca hedged.

"It is."

"I'm at the corporate office in town."

"I'll be there."

Rose said her goodbyes to Portia and went to set her new life in motion.

Twenty minutes later, Rose was being welcomed into Rebecca's arms.

"I was so glad to hear from you," Rebecca said.

Rose looked at Rebecca, and it hit her—this was the last chance to back out. Although, there were no other options. The decision she was about to make would be permanent.

"Don't keep me in suspense, Rose."

"I won't. I just wanted you to know that I thought over your offer," Rose began.

Rebecca held her hand up to stop her from talking.

"Please tell me you decided to take the job. I

already put a bet with Anders, and I told him you'd take this. I told him what you needed was a little time to get everything in a row, but in the end, you would do the reasonable thing."

"Well, I have to tell you, I did go through a lot of tossing and turning before coming to this decision," Rose replied.

"I understand that this company was a dream between you and your late husband. I also know that it takes money to raise twin girls. I—"

"Rebecca, you don't have to sell it to me. I've come to say I'm going to take it."

Rebecca gave a little dance, and then she clasped her hands together. "You won't be sorry that you did this. Once you see how much freedom you have to shape this department, I know you'll be happy."

The one thing that Rose hadn't had a lot of was time. Of course, she understood the practicalities of why she should take this job. Every night as she laid in her bed, she thought about all of the things that Edward probably didn't tell her the truth about. All of those things being equal, she was still attached to this business that had kept her company when her late husband had gone. In some ways, having the cleaning company helped her stay married.

"Well, I'll have to tell Anders, but I want you to know we are completely open to any of the contracts that you already have. If you don't want to bring those contracts, that's fine, too."

"Rebecca, I want to thank you for thinking of me and offering me this opportunity. I'm going to do my very best for you."

"Rose, I'm not insensitive. I can tell that you're

still upset about having to leave the cleaning business."

Rose let out a large sigh and then took a seat in a nearby chair. "You're right, I am still a little bummed out over having to leave the business. I still think of it as something I was preparing for the twins. However, you are giving me a great opportunity to do something new in my life. With all things considered, it might be a better life lesson for me to move on."

"I have confidence in you, Rose. I know you'll do the right thing, so I'm not worried. However, I have to tell you, I can't wait to tell Anders."

Rose decided after she made this epic decision, she needed to ground herself. The people who made her feel the most comfortable and brought her back to what was important were the twins. She gave a call to Traci and told her she would pick the twins up herself. When she arrived at the school, all the kids were doing downward dog. It was true, they didn't all have the yoga pose quite right, but they were trying. In the front of the class was Gloria Danvers. Rose remembered that Portia was trying to help her get a project started. She wondered if it had something to do with yoga.

Rose waited a few more moments, then Gloria Danvers told everyone to stand up and reach for the sky. After the children had finished reaching for the sky, they all dispersed and started running around the classroom. It was hard to believe that not even five minutes ago the room was silent. The twins saw Rose at the front door and came running, talking simultaneously about their day. Gloria walked over, and as soon as she stood next to the girls, they both started to quiet.

"How do you do that?"

Gloria smiled. "I always find that the children will always do the same thing that I'm doing."

Rose wanted to say that that might have been true for Gloria, but it definitely wasn't true for herself. "You just have a touch."

"I'm banking on it."

"Really?"

Gloria nodded. "I don't know if you know, but I've been working with Portia so that I can open up a yoga studio. I want it to be something that specializes in teaching children how to do yoga."

Rose looked around the classroom and then shook her head. "You must really love what you do to decide to be around children all day long, teaching yoga."

"I'm only going to be with them for forty-five minutes at a time. Besides, yoga has done so much for me that I just want to share the experience."

"Have you been practicing yoga for long?"

"I used to work in the city in a very high-powered job that had me flying all over the globe. Essentially, I started to burn out due to my poor life decisions. Yoga helped me to recenter myself and put myself first."

"That sounds so beautiful," Rose said.

Gloria laughed. "I don't want you to think I was on a happy road of enlightenment. I realized I had been doing too much after I had a miscarriage."

"I'm so sorry."

Gloria's smile dimmed a little bit and then she

nodded. "It's not something I would have willingly gone through, but I have to say that it was definitely a turning point in my life to make me look at what was important. It helped me to look at the people in my life to see if they valued what I valued. That's what I like about yoga. It helps you to look at the things and people around you, and you find that the people around you reflect you back. So, when you see the kids all calm around me, that's because I'm calm around them."

Rose gathered the twins up and put them in the car. The twins were veritable chatterboxes the whole way home. On the way, the only thing Rose could really think about was everything Gloria had said.

"Mom?"

Rose came out of her deep thoughts and looked in the rearview mirror to see Anna. "Yes, love?"

"I love you. "

Rose smiled. "Oh, I think I love you more."

Both of the twins giggled. It was a popular game that they played between themselves about who loved the other person more.

"I love you more than candy and marshmallows," Anna said.

"I love you more than ballerinas," Hannah said.

When the car came to a stoplight, Rose looked at the twins through the rearview mirror again.

"That's a lot of loving going on from back there."

"You look sad, so we wanted to let you know you were loved."

"I guess I am, aren't I?"

The rest of the trip, the twins were in deep conversation, talking to one another, but Gloria's words stayed on Rose's mind. She didn't feel so bad about taking the job from Rebecca now. It seemed like even though there was tragedy in life, you could still come out on top. She wasn't going to let Edward's lies destroy her life or the twins'. She was going to find a way, to not only get past it, but to do better for herself and the twins. She was just wondering, what role did Grayson play in all that? Or did he want to play one at all?

CHAPTER 12

Grayson received a text that explained that Hannah was waiting for him to read to her tonight. When he texted Rose, she told him Hannah had a lot of books. She'd read most of them, but she had books. Grayson thought he'd buy her a new book so she wouldn't have to keep rereading the same ones. Mr. Dane had invited him out for dinner tonight unexpectedly. The dinner was supposed to be at six o'clock. Grayson looked at the time and thought he had plenty of time to buy a book. With two hours to spare, certainly, it wouldn't take him that long to get a second-grade story, which was the level Hannah was reading at already.

The nearest local bookstore wasn't that far away from the restaurant he was meeting Mr. Dane at. Being a consummate planner, Grayson thought this was definitely a sign that everything was going to go his way today. When Grayson walked into the bookstore, he was greeted by a blast of cool air and a smiling greeter.

"Hello, welcome to Bay Books."

"Yes, thank you so much. Can you help me out? I'm looking for a book for a five-year-old."

The woman practically preened in front of him.

"Of course, I can. Just follow me, and I will take you to the section."

Grayson became a little leery as they kept walking. What section was she talking about? How much reading were five-year-olds doing these days? After walking past several aisles, they made it to the section that was labeled Elementary and grade school.

Grayson looked at the area and wanted to tell the woman that she had brought him to the wrong place. The section was ginormous. There was a round open section that had several benches in the middle. Next to each bench was easily a pile of six to seven books. On the outer edges of the circle, there were pillows where people could sit. The pillows were grouped into twos and fours. As he moved closer to the circle, he could see that there were bookcases around the circumference. Each one of the bookcases seemed to list a different genre, like science fiction, adventure, science, and more. Grayson turned to look at the young lady, determined to tell her that she had brought him to the wrong place. It was as if she knew what he was thinking when she saw his face.

"Schools are promoting early reading, and as a result, the book section to accommodate those needs has grown. Now children have the same number of options as adults when it comes to reading."

Grayson was overwhelmed. Then he plastered

on his fundraising smile and once again faced the young woman.

"Can you help me out and pick out a book for a five-year-old?"

"Do you know what she likes?"

"She likes ballerinas."

The woman's face lit up. "That's great. Just follow me. We have a whole selection of books about dance."

The woman took off so fast Grayson didn't have a chance to stop her, but he caught up to her in two strides.

"No, I'm sorry. You don't understand. She likes ballerinas, but she doesn't want to dance."

The woman looked completely confused. "How is she going to be a ballerina if she doesn't dance?"

Grayson really wanted to say maybe she should speak to Hannah because he had already brought up this point to Hannah and it didn't seem to make a difference. Not wanting to get into a long-drawn-out discussion as his time was passing by, he wanted to try another tactic. "Do all the books about ballerinas involve dancing?"

The woman looked at him as if he had lost his mind. "That is what ballerinas do, yes."

"How about you give me the top three most popular books for five-year-olds?" The woman looked a little more exasperated, but then she walked over to another bookcase.

"Okay, what level of reader is she?"

Not knowing exactly how to answer this question, Grayson pulled information from the conversation he had with Hannah.

"She's a second-grade reader."

The woman's eyes lit up. "That is so good that she's so far ahead. It shows that you're doing a great job with her. If only more fathers spent time with their children reading."

Grayson didn't try to correct her because, at this point, he just needed the book. Instead of going to another bookcase, the woman walked in the middle of the aisle of the store and brought him in front of a table.

"All of these books are on the Top Twenty To Read list, and they are for second-grade readers. If you pick any of these, I'm sure she'll enjoy it."

After that declaration, the woman left. Grayson looked at the table. All of the books had to be at least two inches thick. He picked up one of the books and flipped through the pages. The book had 240 pages with maybe five pictures in the book total. He wasn't sure he could read this book, much less read it with Hannah.

He wanted to go and ask the woman if she was sure this was the right place, but the woman was already talking to another customer. Grayson had already spent forty minutes in this bookstore. He looked at all the books and then picked the one that had some pink on the cover. Grayson paid for it and left to make the restaurant appointment. He would keep it with him, and after dinner with Mr. Dane, he would go straight over and read the book to Hannah before she went to bed at eight.

As usual, Grayson had everything planned out to the minute. He arrived at the restaurant called The Standard at exactly six o'clock. When he arrived, he received a text from Mr. Dane that said he would be held up this evening. Mr. Dane told him he'd be there around 6:45, and that it was important they meet tonight.

On the way, the only thing that Grayson could think about was the book sitting in his car. At 6:45, Mr. Dane walked into the restaurant. An hour and fifteen minutes wasn't a lot of time in order to eat and have small talk. Grayson could feel his palm starting to get sweaty as he thought about disappointing Hannah.

When Mr. Dane took a seat at the table, he waved away the waiter who came to take their order. Grayson smiled, but he was feeling the pressure of time going by. It was The Standard, a restaurant that only served American fare. Grayson couldn't imagine how much time Mr. Dane would need to look at the menu. However, when the waiter came the second time, Mr. Dane said he would take the appetizers. Grayson didn't order any appetizers. He hoped his lack of involvement in the food would be a hint to Mr. Dane that he really wanted to move this along. If that was his hint, then his hope fell on deaf ears.

"Mr. Dane, I'm thrilled to meet with you, and I'm grateful that you are taking care of my mom's affairs. I just wasn't sure of the reason for the unexpected meeting."

"You know, Grayson, the reason Patti put that stipulation in her will is because she was concerned."

"Concerned?"

"Yes. It seems as though she had met the last person whom you said was your fiancée, and she was concerned that it was not going to be a long-term endeavor. Her thought was that if it fell apart, you would just totally give up on ever finding anyone.

She thought that would have been one of the saddest things ever. Out of all of her sons, you are the one she thought would come home and make a family."

Grayson smiled to himself. Nothing ever got past his mom. She probably knew that the relationship with Sheila wasn't going to work out way before he did. Listening to Mr. Dane, Grayson could also admit to himself that his mom was right. He had been ready to give up on love and just move back to the house where he had all of his best memories. As a fundraiser, he could travel anywhere he wanted in the world and come back home. Grayson had to admit, the home had become the most important ideal to him in the last ten years. His brother Reid had teased him that he was becoming old before his time.

"I want to thank you for sharing that, Mr. Dane."

"I thought you would want to know why she set up her will this way. Actually, I asked Patti to give you a call to explain it before she passed, but she said that it would all take care of itself. Now, let's look at that dessert menu."

Grayson took another peek at his watch, only to find that the time had truly passed. It was 9:15, and he knew he had missed Hannah's bedtime. There was such a heavy weight of guilt on his shoulders he wasn't sure if he would be able to make it through dessert, so he just ordered coffee. Thirty minutes later, Mr. Dane had decided enough was enough and they could both go home. Grayson smiled, but the damage was done. He had let down Hannah. This was the reason he didn't want to meet with children. With children came responsibility, and he hadn't wanted to be like so many others who had been with him before Patti came.

Not wanting to seem like a total loser in her eyes, he decided he would drop the books off in the mailbox. What was he thinking, agreeing to read a story? On the way to Rose's house, he thought about all the times that adults had let him down. He had promised he would never put a child in that same position, yet here he was, sneaking up at night to drop off a book so he wouldn't have to face the consequences of a disappointed child.

The next day, Grayson received photos on his phone of Hannah holding the book, sitting in bed reading it. He wanted to say something but had no idea what to say. Grayson wondered when Rose would call him and tell him he was right, he shouldn't see her kids, and to keep it to business. It was Friday, and normally he would be looking at the restaurants to see where he would be going for the night, but tonight he didn't want to go out. More importantly, Grayson doesn't want to go out alone. Just when he was about to settle himself to watch television, he got a call.

"Bro, I want to celebrate. I'm going to arrive at the Bay tonight, and me, you, and Reid can help me celebrate for a night."

"Vincent?" Grayson asked.

"Yes, it's me, Grayson," Vincent said with a long voice. "You know, the smart brother."

Grayson smiled. While Vincent was never known

for being shy, he was right, he was the smarter brother.

"I have a demo with the government on Saturday morning, but I wanted to get together with you and my other brother, who is not putting his life in danger today to celebrate."

"Just what are we celebrating?"

"Well, you know, I was engaged, and I had her investigated. The investigator came back with a report today only to find out her mother isn't sick. She's never gone to my alma mater, and she was after my money, just like I thought she was."

Grayson had heard this story more than once. Vincent ran a very successful engineering company. He also wasn't too hard to look at. It seemed as though many women thought that he was so involved in being a geek, that he could easily be fooled. Eventually, all of them learned that Vincent not only looked good, but he was also incredibly smart, social, and untrusting.

"So, I'm sorry, what are we celebrating again?"

"We're celebrating that I've managed to escape the snares of another woman."

Grayson wasn't so sure that was something to celebrate. "Did you call Reid already?"

"Yes, I caught him right before he was going on another free solo climb. I took it as a sign that it was the best time for us to meet up and celebrate."

"Okay, why don't I send you the link to a steakhouse, and we'll meet up there?"

Grayson decided to go by the bookstore before he went to see his brothers. It wouldn't make up for things, but he would feel better. Four hours later, Grayson wasn't feeling the same. The first thing he discovered was that the bookstore on the weekend was a madhouse! There were children everywhere, and they all wanted someone to help them, and they didn't care if you were their parent or not.

The last time that he had gone to the bookstore, everything was in its place. He didn't know how long those children had been there, but there were books everywhere. He felt sorry for whoever would have to do the cleanup because it didn't look like those children had spared a single book.

Grayson finally got to the point that he just looked for a child who was about the same age as Hannah and asked her to go pick out two of her favorite books. She wouldn't give up both of those books right away, and Grayson wound up having to read a chapter out of one of those books in order to even get them out of her possession. When Grayson arrived, his brothers had already ordered appetizers.

"What took you so long to get to my party?" Vincent asked.

"Do you see the look that's on that man's face? The question is not what took him so long, but who is she?" Reid asked

"Tell me it isn't true, Grayson. You're supposed to be the most sensible out of all of us. I tell you; I'm celebrating not getting caught, and you're late coming to my party because of a woman."

Nothing ever changed with his brothers. They were always teasing him, and he wouldn't have it any other way. "Well, it is so nice to see you, too, Reid. I heard that you slipped on your last climb, but you look just fine. Vincent, it's also good to see you, too. I saw you made the top one hundred companies to work for."

Reid laughed. "Okay, so maybe we jumped the gun, but Vincent and I want to make sure that while you are here fixing mom's stuff, you aren't being taken advantage of."

Grayson wanted to tell the men about the stipulation in Mom's will, but he just couldn't bring himself to do it. It wasn't that he was embarrassed. He just didn't want that to come back to Rose. Then Vincent tapped his fingers on the table to get his attention.

"Okay, what's her name? I can send it over to my investigator now. By Friday, you'll know her past better than she does."

Grayson waved his brother off. "If I had to investigate a woman, I don't think I would date her," Grayson said.

"Spoken like a true innocent," Vincent commented.

"I don't know, Vincent. I think I'm going to have to agree with Grayson. If you need to investigate her, it doesn't sound like this is going to start out on the right foot anyway."

"You two can live in Lala Land if you want to, but I will never just hook up with a woman without a full background check, and if she wants to be with me, she'll have to agree to a prenup, as well."

Grayson looked at his brother and shook his head. He knew Vincent had been the target of a lot of women, but he hadn't realized how many until now.

"Well, when I look for a woman, she's going to have to be somebody who likes to be daring and adventurous," Reid said.

Grayson looked at his brother and wondered if

that was any better than Vincent needing to research each prospective partner.

"You know, at some point, you're going to have to stop trying to climb every mountain," Grayson said.

"Why? I want to live life to the fullest. I can be safe when I'm dead."

"You know, we're used to your antics, but a woman may have an issue with you risking your life all the time."

Reid shook his head. "She's going to have to take me the way I am. Besides, if she doesn't have a sense of adventure, we won't be compatible anyway."

"Stop stalling, Grayson, and tell us about this woman who made you late," Vincent said.

Grayson realizes there is no way he's going to be able to gloss over Rose. Grayson felt bad having to keep his brothers in the dark. "A couple of weeks ago while I was waiting to talk to Mr. Dane—"

Reid interrupted. "You have to meet up with Mr. Dane for…?"

Grayson sighed. "I didn't want to go into the details or tell the rest of you because I really thought it wasn't necessary. Mom had some conditions that she put in her will before I could take ownership of the house. She knew the rest of you would want to visit but not maintain it."

Both his brothers looked at him, concerned. Vincent was the first one to come out of it. "What kind of conditions, and do you need a lawyer or an investigator?"

Ever suspicious, Vincent, of course, would be the first one to offer help. He had to be very careful at this point. Vincent could get distracted by how dishonest he might think other people could be. Reid was the brother who could always tell when he was hiding something.

"She wanted me to bring Sheila home so we could take possession of the house together."

"So, how did that work out when there was no Sheila?" Reid asked.

"Let's just say it's not a done deal yet," Grayson answered, "And before the both of you offer or ask me, this actually has nothing to do about money at all."

"Why didn't you call us right away? You know we would have been down here in a minute. We could have talked to Mr. Dane."

"Listen, I wanted to be able to take care of this myself, okay? Vincent, you are always trying to make sure that someone doesn't steal your money or investigate someone to make sure they're not trying to take something else from you. And Reid, you are always climbing some cliff or doing some other sport. I couldn't even imagine calling you and breaking your concentration."

Reid looked at Grayson and then shook his head. "It doesn't work that way, little brother. Whenever you need something, you call one of us. There's nothing I'm doing, no mountain that's out there that's more important than family."

"I get it, I messed up. No one died."

Vincent grunts. "I don't know if I'd go that far yet. You were late coming to meet your brothers for some woman."

Reid smiled. "As long as she's super-hot, I'm okay. I would hate to think that I had been put on hold for something less than a ten."

Vincent shook his head. "All the tens are toxic."

"I think both of you have so many issues that I can't wait to see you both fall in love."

Both of his brothers looked at him, and then they laughed out loud.

"I know that Mom thought that as soon as we found the right woman, life would be better for us all. But she just didn't know she was the last of the good batches," Reid said.

"So, what have you done with this woman so far?" Vincent asked.

Grayson was looking around, hoping a waiter would come, but they were all busy. It was probably best to get this over with quickly, sort of like ripping off a Band-Aid. "So, I need to say the first thing right now so we can get it out of the way. She has twin daughters."

"And she still looked hot? Does she have a sister?" Reid asked.

"Dude!" Vincent said then he focused back on Grayson. "I thought you had a standing rule about going out with women who have kids."

"It's not what you're thinking, Vincent," Grayson said.

"I don't know. You were late to see your brothers. This woman has kids. It seems like you are breaking all types of rules by being with this woman. What else have you done with her?"

"I haven't really done anything with her. If anything, it's probably very clear why I shouldn't be hanging around her that often. I was supposed to read her daughter a bedtime story, but Mr. Dane wanted to talk, and I had to make sure that everything was okay with Mom's house."

Both of his brothers looked at one another, and then the waiter came. When the waiter had finished taking the orders, he looked at his brothers. "Okay, say something."

"I guess I don't really know what to say, Grayson," Reid said. "We've always known that you were probably going to be the first one to get married if any of us get married. We want to make sure that you run into a nice person who's going to treat you right, and it seems like this girl that you're seeing now has already gotten under your skin."

"I don't know if I think she is the one for you, but I have to agree with Reid when I say you are acting differently than you have with any other woman we've seen so far."

Just then, Grayson was saved by the waiter who brought his appetizers. When Grayson didn't respond to the question right away, his brothers dropped the subject. It was two hours later after they had gotten caught up on everything they'd been doing since they last saw each other that the subject even came up again. Grayson had excused himself to go to the men's room, and when he came back, he felt as though the tone of the table had changed.

"What's wrong?"

Reid sighed and splayed his hands out. "We're worried about you, little brother. You know, we'd do anything for you, and we couldn't be closer if we were blood-related."

"Oh, I feel like if you need to say all of that before you say anything, you're about to say something really harsh," Grayson said.

Vincent cleared his throat. "I just want to say that whatever Reid is going to say is all Reid. I personally believe you should enjoy the moment. It's going to end soon enough. So, enjoy life. You can go on, Reid."

Reid scowled at Vincent and then looked back at Grayson.

"I think you need to be careful, Grayson. I think the idea that this woman is able to get you to date her and she's got twins is pretty telling."

"I'm not dating her. I've seen her a couple of times. It's a small town. You both know that."

"We understand. We're just saying that if a woman can get you to take one or two steps, it's not that far before you're jumping off the cliff.

Grayson laughed. "You two act as if I'm on the shelf, trying to make a last-ditch effort to find someone to spend forever with."

Reid shrugged. "You were always the more sympathetic brother. The only thing we're saying is to be careful. We don't want you to be hurt."

"I hear you, and I want you two to know that I'm not looking for Ms. Right. I'm just trying to settle myself in Mom's house and get my bearings in my business. I need to decide if I am going to run my business from here or if will I have to maintain two offices."

His brothers nodded, and the conversation drifted off to other topics, but Grayson wasn't as sure about what he said. When he thought about his business, it was clear there was no room to do anything but settle in. However, when he thought about the twins and Rose, all of a sudden, they didn't seem like such an imposition.

CHAPTER 13

*T*oday was Review Finances Day with Portia. Besides being Rose's best friend, she was also her financial consultant. She knew all there was to know about what Edward had done and the financial predicament it had put Rose in. As they were wrapping up, Portia tapped Rose's phone.

"For someone in a whirlwind romance with a new hot guy, your phone has been pretty silent. I mean, this is the googly eye stage when you think the way you breathe is romantic," Portia said.

Rose wanted to say she thought that's where she was at, as well. "Maybe I misjudged what was going on."

"So, are you going to call him and straighten this out?" Portia asked.

Calling Grayson. Why should she have to call him? She hadn't done anything wrong. Rose was conflicted about even reaching out to Grayson. Maybe he had decided that they were just going to see each other around Mr. Dane, and that was it. It was a shame if that was the decision he had come to, because Hannah really did like the book.

"Earth to Rose."

"Look, I just think, after Edward that I'm not ready to run after a man."

"Wow, making a phone call is running after a man? Men must think that I'm a stalker when I'm just calling to confirm where we are going to meet for dinner."

Rose rolled her eyes.

"I must be getting close to the problem. You can't even use your words anymore."

"Can we call this a day? I don't think I can focus on the numbers anyway."

Portia nodded and packed up. "Hey, Rose. Remember I'm on your side. If you need anything, just let me know."

Rose was so grateful for her friends, and she gave Portia a big hug. Traci brought the kids back that afternoon to pick up some clothes because they were going to stay at Traci's and have a sleepover with Sophia. The doorbell rang, and Rose looked around to see what was left by Traci or the twins. Instead, she saw Portia's pad. She usually took everything.

"I've got what you're looking for—" Rose said as she opened the door.

Grayson was standing on the other side with his eyebrow raised.

"Well, that is definitely better than the greeting I was expecting," Grayson said.

"Why are you here?" Rose asked.

"I was hoping to get a second shot at a date with

you. One where we do some connecting, and I work on being a better fake fiancée."

"You haven't called at all, and now you just show up? What happens if I have a date already or I have plans?" she asked.

"If there is another man trying to poach on my fiancée, I will slay him with my words," Grayson said gallantly. "You know, that is a perk of being a fundraiser, I know a lot of words, like big three-syllable words."

Rose smirked at his silliness.

"If you have plans to go out with another, then I've arrived just in time to stop this dastardly deed. My chariot awaits you," he said, extending his arm.

"Come in while I find some jeans to put on." Rose widened the door and let Grayson step in. He looked unsure of himself. He had a bouquet of flowers and what looked like a gold box of chocolate. How long had it been since a man had brought Rose gifts? Every time Edward had brought her gifts, she knew he had done something wrong. But to get a gift for no reason at all was a new experience. "You've got gifts in hand, and so this tells me you weren't really sure I'd want to see you."

"It's true. I wasn't."

Rose was confused, and it must have shown on her face." Help me out, Grayson."

"How am I supposed to come and read a bedtime story to Hannah when I missed the time and the appointment? Mr. Dane had called me to a late, unexpected dinner. And I couldn't get out of it."

"You know these things happen, right?"

"What I know is I promised her I would do something, and I wasn't here to fulfill that promise."

Rose waved him off. "Hannah isn't some fragile little girl. She understands that you try to do it, and you weren't able to make it. But you did drop off a book that she really likes to read. I'm curious, where did you get the book from?"

"I had to go to a bookstore, and it was definitely a different experience than what I thought it would be."

Rose smiled. "She was very happy and very surprised that you had something from the bestseller list."

Grayson looked as if he couldn't believe what was being said. "I was wondering if we could stay in and have Chinese delivered. I would like to spend some time with you."

Rose heard the words and was as if she were transported to high school and the guy she liked finally acknowledged her. Portia was right. It was the googly stage.

"Okay, I'll get the menus so we can pick."

"Bring your favorite place, and I'll pick from that. I can literally eat from anywhere."

"Okay, we're going to order from the Golden House."

Grayson looked at her and smiled.

"Not a word from you. If only you had been more talkative, we could have been going out, but no, you decided to keep everything to yourself. That means we eat from the Golden House, and we're all happy."

"Yes, ma'am."

After she placed the order, she went to sit next to him on the couch. A few seconds later, she heard her phone ring. It was a text, but she couldn't just not look at it. When Rose did look at it, she looked back at Grayson and was appalled.

"What did you do?"

"I sent you a Zelle."

"I know what Zelle is. The question is, why did you send it to me?"

Grayson looked totally confused. "Let's try to go over these events so that we're both on the same page, okay, Rose? I came over because I felt as though I had dropped the ball. I wanted to make up for it by taking you out, but instead thought you might be more comfortable staying indoors and I wanted to get to know you. We are getting ready to have dinner, and you paid for it, so I sent you the money so it wouldn't come out of your pocket."

Rose looked at him as if he had lost his mind.

"Grayson, we are having Chinese food. The day that a Chinese delivery dinner for two people is $120 is the day I will stop eating Chinese food."

Grayson shrugged. "Better safe than sorry."

"I'm going to have to send it back to you," Rose said.

"That's going to be unfortunate because I'm going to have to send it back to you."

"Grayson, be reasonable!"

"Rose. Let me be the man."

Normally, she would have had a quick rebuttal. If she were honest, Edward had often said the same thing to her. He would make the odd comment that she was a better man than he could ever be. In retrospect, it was never Rose's intention to offend Edward or Grayson. She just didn't want to be in debt to anyone, and she wanted to make sure things got done.

"Listen, Rose. Let me pay for tonight's dinner, and I will find something that you can pay for the next time."

The next time. He was so sure there was going to be the next time.

"Dinner with Mr. Dane?

"Enlightening."

"Okay, I can see we're going to be cryptic tonight."

Grayson sighed. "My mom knew me really well. It just accentuates how much I'm really going to miss her."

Rose sat next to Grayson and placed her hand on his. "I can tell you she loved you and all of your brothers so much. It was the only thing she could ever talk about whenever I came into the house. If it wasn't one thing, it was another about how well you all were doing. New accomplishments you were making. She was beyond proud of all of you."

"Thanks. You always hope that your parents will think the best of you, but you never know, right?"

Rose thought about her mother. Somewhere out there. She'd never know what her mother thought about her now, either. Although, if she called her mother now, she'd probably ask for something rather than ask how she and the twins were doing.

Twenty minutes later, the doorbell rang, and it was Chinese food. Grayson took the food into the kitchen and set out plates so they could eat at the table. When everything was laid out, he served her.

"You don't have to serve me," Rose said.

Grayson sat back and looked at Rose.

"I think we need to get something straight."

Rose couldn't think of a single conversation that had ever gone right when they started this way.

"Okay."

"You do know that I find you attractive, right?"

"I know you want me to help you by being your fiancée."

"No, I mean even besides that, Rose Sallow, I find you attractive."

"Oh!"

"The first time we met at the restaurant at the bar, I thought that you were an intriguing and amazing woman then. It's true, I thought you were going to do something else for me, but it doesn't matter. What matters is that I still think you are an amazing woman. I know about the hardships you're facing and how you're able to still move on and do what's best for you and your kids. All of your actions only emphasize how incredible you are, and that's why I admire and respect you as a woman."

"Thank you."

"I'd like you to let me take the opportunity to try to court you. I'm one of those old-fashioned guys who still believe in pulling out seats and opening doors to cars. I know it may not be very popular with other people, but my mother taught me those manners, and I hold on more to them now that she's gone."

Rose was humbled by his words and nodded, not sure what else to do.

"So, I've been walking around with this in my pocket, but it's yours."

He pulled out a ring box, and inside was a simple

gold band. Rose looked at it and then him and shook her head.

Grayson smiled. "Wow, you must think I'm really cheap or really poor. Did you think Mr. Dane would believe it if I didn't get my fiancée a ring? What do you think?"

CHAPTER 14

*H*e watched her put it on tentatively before she spoke.

"You didn't have to, but since you did, it's beautiful."

Grayson smiled, and something in him warmed, watching her look at the ring on her hand. This was all make-believe. He had been honest with Rose when he said he really admired her and thought she was attractive, but he was done with the idea of happily ever after, right?

"In the words of illustrious women everywhere, now that I've put a ring on it, I want to know some things."

"Okay, maybe the ring will get you some answers," Rose joked.

"Okay, what is your favorite color?" Grayson asked.

"Purple."

"What's your favorite flower?"

"Amaryllis."

"Uh, what?"

"It's amaryllis. They're beautiful flowers, and they look like big trumpets."

Grayson gave her a look like he wasn't sure about it, but he accepted the answer.

"What's your favorite dessert?"

"Carrot cake."

"Carrot cake?"

"You know this isn't going to get very far if you keep questioning all of my answers," Rose said.

"Fine, what's the thing you like the most about me?"

Grayson looked at Rose, and watched as she was just temporarily stumped into silence.

"What?"

"What do you like about me?"

"Well, what do you mean? What do I like about you? I mean, what do I like about how you look, or what, do I like about how you act?"

"I didn't realize it was such a difficult question."

"It's not a difficult question."

"Okay, then tell me what it is that you like about how I look?"

Rose put her fork down and then glared at Grayson.

"I don't think I should be the only one answering these questions. I don't know the answers to the questions that you've asked me."

Grayson smiled.

"You're stalling, but I respect that. My favorite color is black. It hides all stains. My favorite flower? Fake ones. They never die, and they're reusable. And my favorite dessert? Hands down, it's cheesecake.

Okay, now you know all the things I know about you. It's your turn."

Rose cleared her throat.

"Well. I think you have good teeth."

"What?"

"Good teeth are very important. The only thing more important than good teeth is a person with good hair."

Grayson began to laugh. He could barely contain himself on the seat.

"I have to tell you, Rose, that is a first. So, you've obviously given this some thought. Would you like to tell me why my teeth and hair are important? At this rate, I feel like if I only had a tail, you'd be happier."

"No, silly. It's just that when someone takes care of their teeth and hair, it tells you about their whole body. There's nothing worse than looking at someone who looked very attractive and fit, and then when you get ready to touch them, they fall over, or they don't have as much strength as you think they do."

"I feel like there's a story behind this."

"I'm just saying that once upon a time before I got married to Edward, I used to want to go out with this guy. Finally, he said that we were going to go out, and I could pick the place. I picked going on an easy trail walk. He could barely make it up the trail, much less back. That's when I realized just because it looked good on the outside, if the teeth in the hair aren't right, it's a no-go."

"Okay. Well, I'm glad I passed the teeth and hair test."

"You can laugh, but I'm telling you it's important."

The next couple of hours passed quickly. Grayson and Rose spoke about everything they could think of under the sun. He talked about how he loved doing his job and how being able to raise money for charities was one of the most purposeful things in his life. Rose spoke about how she loved being a mother. Having the twins was the most life-changing event in her life and the one that she wouldn't change for anything.

When the both of them realized that darkness had settled outside, Grayson knew it was time for him to go. Rose walked him to the door.

"I want to thank you for coming by tonight, Grayson. It really meant a lot to me. And I had a lot of fun."

"I want to thank you for forgiving me for missing my appointment. I'm still not sure if I believe the whole teeth-and-hair thing, but I'll let you get away with it this time."

The both of them laughed, and there was this air of expectancy between the both of them. Rose put her hand on the doorknob to open the door, and Grayson put his hand on top of hers.

"I know that we are just pretending to be together, but I'd like to ask something."

"Go ahead," Rose said in a low voice.

"Would you mind if I kissed you, Rose Sallow?"

Rose looked up at him and cut her head to the side.

"You know, I've been wondering when we were going to do this, and I have to tell you, I have some reservations."

Grayson couldn't contain the smile on his face.

"I see my ego is going to be taking a beating as we go through this relationship."

"It's not you, Grayson."

Both of his hands went to his heart, and then his right hand went to his forehead in a dramatic flair.

"Please, oh please, don't say the 'it's not you, it's me thing."

Rose laughed. "Maybe. I don't know. What I do know is I've been dreading kissing you because I don't even know if I remember how to do this."

"You don't forget how to kiss people."

"Well, let me tell you, I've been kissing the girls, and somehow I don't think you want me to blow raspberries on your cheeks and then give you a kiss."

"I'm not so much into the raspberries." Grayson reached for both of her hands and put them into his and then looked into her eyes.

"This isn't a test, Rose. This is just me. A man who has found an incredibly beautiful woman who has such a strength of character he never thought to find. I'd just like to kiss that beautiful woman."

Rose looked at him, dazed. "I'm not sure I agree with what you see, but I am all for you kissing me."

Grayson let her hands go and then took his hands and framed her neck. His hands traveled up her neck until he tilted back her head and then bent down and kissed her. There was no rush on his side. He could still taste the sweet sauce from her dinner. He didn't push her for more. He just wanted to know what it was like to kiss Rose Sallow. Grayson lifted his head and looked down into a smiling face.

"Was it enough?" she asked.

Grayson smiled. "It was for tonight. Get some

rest. You've got to prepare yourself to be my fiancée."

"What does that mean?" Rose asked suspiciously.

Grayson laughed and then gave her a quick peck on her cheek. "I don't know what kind of man you thought I was, but as I said, I'm not cheap or poor. Goodnight, Rose. Dream of me."

As Grayson was driving away, the only thing he could think of was when he met with his brothers. He had joked with them that he wasn't going to fall in love. He told them that he and Rose were entirely too sensible to do something like that. Now he wasn't so sure.

CHAPTER 15

The man was relentless, and she had no idea how he got his information. Those were the thoughts that were going through Rose's head as she went to answer the door. It all started on Monday morning. At nine o'clock, a man showed up with amaryllises. The first one was endearing, but then they came every hour on the hour until one o'clock in the afternoon. It was true, they were all different colors and Rose oohed and ahhed over each one. At the same time, she said how silly and wasteful it was for Grayson to send them. Then when the twins came home and asked about the flowers, she had to field questions from Hannah, Anna, and Traci about how Grayson was just being nice.

Rose was grateful she hadn't put the ring on her finger. She was hoping she wouldn't have to tell anyone, and that way it wouldn't be an issue when the "engagement" was over. On Tuesday, nothing happened, and Rose thought that Grayson's antics were over. That couldn't have been further from the truth. On Wednesday morning, a ballerina came to the door and invited the girls and Rose to go school shopping. Grayson would come later that evening, and they would all go out in order to get school supplies since they were going to a new school. The girls thought it was amazing. Hannah was enthralled with the delivery woman. The whole time the ballerina was there, she never danced once.

And that was how Rose found herself opening her door at 4:30 in the afternoon on a Wednesday to go out with Grayson to go shopping and to take the girls out to eat afterwards, of course.

"You know you're crazy, right?" Rose said.

"I could say the same thing about you waiting until the last moment to get school supplies. All of the best stuff will be gone."

Rose looked at him and shook her head. "It doesn't work like that. The store never ran out of pencils, pens, and papers."

"But they might run out of ballerina ones."

A resounding yes echoed in the background, and Rose had to close her eyes and let the moment pass through her. Hannah came running around her, dragging Anna behind her.

"I need you to meet my sister, Anna," Hannah said to Grayson.

"Okay."

"You don't understand. We can't talk to strangers, and I have already met you. Anna didn't meet you yet."

"Ah, I get it. Well, Miss Anna, my name is Grayson, and I'm a friend of Hannah's."

Rose looked as Anna peeked around Hannah and gave Grayson a small smile.

"Hi, Grayson," Anna practically whispered. It always amazed Rose how the twins were so different. It was true they looked like each other, but Hannah had an outgoing personality that couldn't be contained. Anna, on the other side, was everything quiet.

"So, ladies, are you ready to go to the store and get some bare necessities?" Grayson said, wiggling his eyebrows. The twins laughed and inevitably they started singing the song "Bare Necessities" from Jungle Book. Rose thought if she could just survive an hour she'd be fine. She didn't think that Grayson could actually keep this up. Rose was going to give him an hour, and then when she saw him getting ready to fray at the edges, she would save him. At least, that was the plan.

When everyone got into Grayson's car, he asked them what they wanted to buy. Rose looked at him as if he'd lost his mind. Hannah took the opportunity to be the spokesperson for both her and her twin, saying all the things she would like to have.

"That's a pretty extensive list, Hannah," Grayson said.

Was he starting to get a hint of how big of a task he was taking on?

"No worries. We have plenty of time to walk the aisles, and I'm sure we'll find everything that you're looking for."

Rose turned and looked at him, and she couldn't believe the words that had come out of his mouth.

"Maybe we should have a little moderation. Let's think about what we want to buy because we have a budget," Rose said, trying to interject some form of sanity into this experience.

"Oh yeah, that's right. The budget," Grayson said in a conspiratorial tone. "Hannah, what do you think about the budget?"

Hannah wasn't one to let an opportunity go by. "I think we should put a lot of money in the budget," she said solemnly.

Grayson nodded as he drove. "That sounds like a sound plan. Okay, everybody, let's all vote on it. Who thinks we should put a lot of money in the budget?"

Both of the twins said yes, as well as Grayson. When they came to a stop light, Rose tapped Grayson on the hand to get his attention. "That's not how a budget works," she whispered

"Let's just see where it takes us," Grayson said as if he didn't have a care in the world.

"Can I go shopping with my friend Grayson?" Hannah asked as they pulled into the parking lot. Rose looked at Grayson. Could he handle it? The store wasn't that big. It was a one-floor department store. Hannah was also wearing her GPS pin.

Grayson reached over, and Rose's eyes went to his.

"Rose, we can all stay together. I don't mind."

"Mom?" Hannah asked from the backseat.

She would be perfectly safe in the store with Grayson. This was just one more step she needed to take as things were moving along in life. She didn't want to hold Hannah back. Throwing her shoulders back, she looked at the rearview mirror.

"Okay, you can shop with Grayson, but we all set our watches and we meet back in forty-five minutes. Deal?"

Hannah was practically jumping out of her seat.

"Deal, and thank you, thank you, thank you so much, Mom," Hannah effused. Then Hannah turned to Grayson. "I really need a book bag."

Rose looked at her in disbelief. "What is wrong with your book bag?" Rose asked.

"It looked just like Anna's. In the morning, we get them confused," Hannah whined.

"So why don't we just put your name on one of them?" Rose asked. When Hannah didn't look as though she liked that answer, Rose turned to Grayson. "Okay, it's your turn to weigh in. What do you think?"

Rose watched Hannah perk up a bit. Grayson would say the right thing, and then Hannah would understand how things worked.

Grayson cleared his throat. "I think that your mother has a great idea when she said you should put your name on your book bag. Even if your bookbag didn't look like your sister's, I still think you should put your name on your bookbag. However, since we are already here at the store, there's no reason for us not to pick up another bag. If we had to go out of our way, maybe we wouldn't, but since we're already here, I think it's a great idea."

Hannah put her hands over her mouth and screamed in joy. Her little feet were flailing sitting in the car seat. Rose just shook her head and turned back around to face the front.

"Grayson, I can't believe you're encouraging her like this," Rose said, with no heat in her words.

"I'm trying to make sure that I'm the good guy. Now, I think we all need to get together so we can hit the store running and then go get some food."

Rose saw Hannah put her hand into Grayson's, and they began to walk down one of the aisles. At that moment, Rose tried to remember the last time that Edward had walked down one with one of the twins. Rose tried to remember when Edward had spent any time with the twins, and nothing came to her. Grayson said he didn't want to be around kids and didn't want them to become attached to him, but it was clear the attachment he was trying to protect himself against went both ways.

For her, it wasn't even a question. Rose Sallow was falling for Grayson Chance hard.

Hannah and Grayson spent a lot of time looking at book bags. Eventually, Hannah picked up a bag for herself but said she wouldn't feel right if she got a bag and Anna didn't.

"What does Anna like?"

"She likes dogs."

"Don't you like dogs?"

Hannah shook her head. "They're so big and messy, and my mom said that no matter what you do, they always need help going to the bathroom."

Grayson laughed. "That's kind of true. When I was growing up, I always wanted a pet of my own."

"Your mom didn't want you to have one?"

"My mom knew I wasn't going to take care of it."

"Oh, your mom sounds really smart. Chemistry is where you have to be really smart, too."

"I'd like to think so, Hannah."

They kept walking around the store, and every so often, Grayson looked at his watch, making sure they had enough time to get back to where they needed to meet Rose. Finally, Hannah found a book bag that she was pretty sure Anna would like, as well. Right before she put it into the basket, she turned and faced Grayson.

"What's wrong, Hannah?"

"Do we have a really big budget?" she asked.

"I think it's really big. Why? Is there something that you want?"

"Do we have enough in the budget that I can get you to stay with us?"

Grayson froze and looked at Hannah. "What did you say, Hannah?"

"Everybody else is going to go to the first day of school with a mom and a dad. Can you go with us on our first day?"

Grayson stopped, and all of his fears came crashing in. Wasn't this what he was trying not to do? How could he have been so wrapped up in him and Rose that he forgot who the most important people in this situation were? He looked at his watch, and there was still fifteen minutes to go. He had no clue what to say.

"Hannah, you don't need a budget for that. I think you are an amazing girl. I want you to know that if I'm in town, I will go with you on the first day of school."

"Some of the kids in my class are going to go to my school, too. They are all talking about what their mom and dad are going to do for them and how both of their parents are going to bring them to school. I just don't want to be alone."

"Let me work on it and talk to your mom. You know your mom is soooo amazing. Even if I can't go,

I want you to know the other kids don't have an amazing mom like yours."

"You're right. My mom is amazing. Okay. So, we talked about everybody else, but, Grayson, you didn't say what you wanted."

"You know, I have been wondering the same thing."

"Do you need help picking? We can get you a book bag, too."

"I don't think I need a book bag, but I will find something to put in the cart."

"Grayson, I just want you to know that even if you can't come for my first day, you would be really good at going to somebody else's first day."

"You think so?"

Hannah nodded. "I listen to all the other kids, and they say that their dad gives them everything, just like you did today."

Grayson had to look at the ground and clear his throat to be able to look at her. How could it be that this little girl could make him speechless and bring him to his knees? Fortunately, it was time to go.

"Thank you so much, Hannah. Now, let's get back so that your mom doesn't worry."

"That's so true. She worries over everything."

"It's the sign of a loving mother."

"Then she loves us more than any other mom in the world," Hannah moaned.

Grayson brought Hannah back to their meetup spot, and they finally got to the cash register. After everything was rung up, Rose went into her purse to retrieve her card, but Grayson told the cashier to put everything on his card.

Rose started to protest. "Grayson, what are you doing?"

"I'm not doing anything now. I've already paid." Before Rose could get the check, Grayson had already pocketed the receipt. As everything was being loaded up into the car, Rose said she would pay for dinner. Grayson wanted to tell her it was okay and that he had it, but Rose wasn't listening, and he didn't want to argue with her. This might be the last time they were together.

CHAPTER 16

*A*fter everyone was in the car, Rose asked the magic question that she knew the answer to and dreaded.

"Where do you all want to go and eat?"

Hannah and Anna both said in unison, "The ball house!"

Grayson looked at Rose with a smile on his face. "I'm not familiar with this place of fine dining," he said with a smile.

Rose shook her head and sighed. "No adult is familiar with this place. However, I think you would be hard-pressed to find any kid who doesn't know what it is."

"If you can direct me to get me there, we can go."

Rose nodded and gave him directions to the ball house. As soon as they got into the ball house, Hannah went and talked to Anna. Then Anna dropped Rose's hand and went to sit next to Grayson. Grayson smiled at her and then asked what she would like to eat. She would get to decide for the whole family, and Rose once again couldn't see how Grayson could let the girls just wrap him around their fingers. To make sure that something would come out of the kitchen she could eat, Rose escorted Hannah to the table just in time to hear Anna place an order for pizza.

"I think pizza is a great idea, Anna."

Shy Anna smiled but shook her head.

"This must be all your idea because Mommy only brings us here on very, very special occasions."

Just then, Grayson looked up and saw Rose smirking at him.

Here was a man who had so much to give, and Rose had to admit that she thought the both of them were scared to reach out and grab what could be between them.

"They'll bring the pizza to the table, so if you want, you can go look around," Rose said.

Anna didn't have to be told twice. The twins ran off, and before long, they were lost in the crowd of children jumping into ball pits.

"I think today is going pretty well. What do you think?"

Rose turned to look at Grayson. What did she think? If she were honest, she would say she'd barely had time to think since he'd launched this I-am-your-fiancé campaign. Rose felt like this question was way more than just how the day was going. She could see a distant and reserved look coming into Grayson's eyes, and she wasn't sure why.

"Grayson, do you know what we're doing here?"

He turned to her and nodded. "You know, Rose, it was so hard growing up in foster homes. As a kid, I never thought going to a new home was a problem. I could make up all sorts of stories about why I needed to travel from home to home. I could never come up with a good reason for disappointment or why people didn't fulfill their promises. I didn't want to be in that group."

Rose placed her hand over Grayson's.

"I may not understand exactly the disappointment that you're talking about. However, I have to tell you that's not you, Grayson."

"How could it not be if that's the only example that I've ever had? Maybe that's already in my genes, and I can't really change it."

"Grayson, if that were true, what you would be saying is the only times people could be good parents would be if they came from good parents."

"I'm not saying that. I'm saying that children deserve a certain amount of dedication and attention because they give you their trust."

Rose wanted to explain to him that it wasn't one thing or another. She wanted to explain to him that being a parent was a complex affair and that all parents wished the world were black and white, but it wasn't. She wanted to explain to him that when they were together, it was complicated on her end, but she was starting to think it was worth the effort to figure it out. The evening ended all too soon for the twins. After they had been packed up in the car, Grayson drove them all home. He helped Rose bring them in, and when he got ready to lay Hannah down, she grabbed onto his neck.

"Can you stay?" Hannah asked. Rose saw the moment of hesitation on Grayson's face.

"What do you want to do, Hannah?" Grayson asked, for once being a little cautious.

"Mommy bought a bunch of videos, and one of them is called Sally's First Day of School."

Grayson nodded sagely. "Of course, I'll watch it with you."

Rose saw how Hannah asked with her inside voice so that she wasn't too loud. Hannah following the rules about asking for things was a sign of Hannah getting to like Grayson. She'd have a talk with the girls when Grayson left. Rose wasn't oblivious to how Hannah had started to like Grayson, but she also knew she couldn't keep Hannah in a bubble, and she'd have to learn that some people come and go in her life, and it was okay.

"Sally has a new book bag, too," Hannah said.

"I have a very old bag that I take to work," Grayson said.

"Maybe we should get you a bag, so some people won't make fun of you when you go to work," Hannah said.

"When I go to work, I usually have to tell everybody what to do, so they don't make fun of me."

"Oh, you mean you're like the teachers, huh?"

"Something like that."

Rose loaded up the video, and then everyone sat on the couch. Hannah started talking almost right away. Rose smiled, hoping that Grayson didn't think he was going to actually be able to watch the video. Rose felt a little tug on her side. It was Hannah.

"I think I like all of us being here."

Rose took a quick glimpse at Grayson, whose head was bent low as he spoke to Anna.

"You know, munchkin? I think I like it, too."

They waited until the video was over. Miraculously, both of the twins fell asleep. After Grayson had helped her put the twins in bed, she came out, hoping to have a conversation, but it was cut short.

"Grayson, I wanted to talk about–"

"Rose, I wanted to talk, too, but I don't think this is the right time."

Rose couldn't have been more shocked or hurt. She thought the day had gone well.

"I understand. And, you know, if you could just send me the bill for today, I'll make sure to take care of it."

"The bill is on me. It's all part of me taking care of my fiancée. Today was everything I thought it would be, and I just need some time to think about that."

"Do you want to talk about it?"

Grayson ran his hands through his hair and let out a huge sigh.

"No, I'm sorry. I just need to get my thoughts together. I need to go."

"Grayson."

"I'm sorry. I just need to go."

Rose watched Grayson walk out the door and she felt like she should stop him, but she wasn't that woman. She wasn't going to beg him to stay. If he wanted to go, then it was fine with her. If she said it a couple hundred more times, she'd believe it.

CHAPTER 17

$\mathcal{G}$rayson was going to call it off that morning, but then Mr. Dane called. He wanted to see him and his fiancée tonight.

CAN YOU MAKE IT OUT TONIGHT? IT'S SHOWTIME.

OF COURSE.

MEET YOU AT THE STANDARD STEAKHOUSE.

GREAT, SEE YOU THERE.

When Grayson saw Rose walk up to the restaurant in a red sheath dress, he had to stop talking on the phone. He could see several other men looking at Rose, and he felt an unexpected pang of jealousy. Not that he had a right to feel jealous anymore. He had already decided that whatever this was between them was over.

"When Mr. Dane sees you, he's not going to wonder why I kept you to myself."

Rose held up her ring finger with the gold band around it.

"I wanted to make sure I presented myself as someone you'd actually be with."

Grayson wanted to say something, but then it was time.

"I wonder why Mr. Dane wanted to meet here. It's not like it's exactly what I would call an out-of-the-way spot," Rose said.

The host took them to their table. The first thing that Grayson noticed was that the table was off to the side in a cozy corner. This night was going further and further away from what Grayson had intended it to be. When he looked over at Rose, he was filled with indecision about their relationship. An uncomfortable silence settled on the table.

"When did Mr. Dane call you?" Rose asked.

"He actually called me first thing this morning, saying he had an opening."

"I didn't realize his business was so busy."

Once again, the conversation dwindled into an awkwardness. Once again the hostess came to the table.

"Hello. Mr. Dane said he is a bit delayed and that you can get started without him," the woman said before disappearing into the interior of the restaurant. This wasn't going according to plan at all.

"Have you been here before?" Rose asked.

Grayson settled in for the long haul because this was going to be a long night.

"The surf and turf is usually good here. I'm not one for trying new things. Usually, when I find something I like, I stick with it," Grayson said. There was some light chatter that went on between them, every sentence seeming more cautious than the last.

Eventually, the meal was over, and Mr. Dane hadn't shown up.

"You know, I wanted to ask you something if you don't mind," Rose said.

"Go for it." In fact, he thought she should keep on talking until he found a way to break up with her.

"Why didn't you ask your ex to do this?"

For a moment, Grayson was totally stunned. "Ask Sheila? She's a nice person, but I think there were things that were big hurdles for us that made it so that we couldn't be friends afterward."

"Wow, I'm sorry. I didn't mean to bring up bad memories."

Grayson heard her and he didn't have to explain anything, but he still thought he needed to in order to have some sort of closure.

"Sheila didn't want the family, moving to Inheritance Bay, and the whole dream," Grayson said.

"I know family is very important to you," Rose said cautiously. "You two couldn't work it out?"

"No, there wasn't anything to work out. Family and kids were a big part of what I was looking for, and she didn't want to have them or to entertain a family, unless we accidentally had one, I suppose. I like to plan important things better than that."

"Did she have kids?"

"No, she didn't."

"It seems like we all have those moments where we have lines we just won't cross," she said.

"I think no matter the person, they have some things they cling to. I mean, I see you devote yourself to the twins, but you practically ignore yourself. If you do consider yourself, it's to sacrifice yourself for the kids, whether they need it or not."

Rose shook her head. "That's different. That's what parents do."

Grayson nodded. "You're right, parents do sacrifice for their kids when they need to. My mom sacrificed for us because the funds were low. You were going to stay with the cleaning company for what? If the girls didn't like it, then they would be stuck with a legacy albatross."

Rose took her napkin and placed it on the table.

"An albatross? Of course, they would have loved the company and stayed with it."

"No, one girl loves ballerinas and the other dogs. I'm not sure how you can be so sure either one would want a cleaning company."

The look on Rose's face stopped Grayson, and he reached out to touch her hand to apologize, and she pulled it back from him.

"You don't understand kids, Grayson. It's true you might have been a kid, but you lost the kid view a long time ago. So, you'll forgive me if I can't take the words of a man who supposedly ran from kids but is so at home with them."

Grayson gritted his teeth. He wasn't the one doing wrong here. He was trying to look out for the twins. He wanted to save them from the pain he had gone through time and time again.

"I'm sorry I brought it up. Hannah asked me to go to the first day of school with her."

Rose looked shocked and then looked away. Right when Grayson was going to say something, the host came over with a tray of coffee and carrot cake.

"Mr. Dane said he was sorry he missed this appointment and sends his regrets."

When the hostess left, Rose attacked the carrot cake and said nothing. When the cake and coffee were gone, she sat back and looked at Grayson as if she were having deep thoughts.

"I wonder, Grayson, what would you have me do? Do you think I should run out and find just any man to be with me and my kids?" Rose asked.

"No. I'm not saying that at all. However, I think you need to remember that if you don't care for yourself, you can't care for the people around you."

"I suppose that's great advice from a man who's too scared to have people around who love him. Anytime anyone gets too close, you run away."

"I'm not running. I'm being responsible. If I want to continue to be responsible, I have to tell you that I'm not going to be able to do the fake fiancé thing or see you. It's for the best."

"You know what, I guess you would think it's for the best. You don't have to risk your feelings anymore."

"I was wrong. I should have done this before we came to the restaurant."

"Well, don't worry. I won't take up any more of your time." Rose stood up and left the restaurant.

After a rousing fight, and a public breakup, Rose woke to a message from Jonathan, saying the sale was final and he'd be by to drop off the paperwork. Yes, her life was going just perfectly. Rose made it to her office, and she was happy that Traci hadn't arrived yet. She should be happy, all things considered. In about a week, her girls would be leaving pre-k and going to kindergarten for the first time. They were excited and prepared, thanks to Grayson, whom she didn't even want to think about now. Rose decided she would go home right after Jonathan left. She could leave a note for Traci and then try to sleep off the depression that was surely coming.

What was making things even worse were she woke up with the engagement ring on her finger. It was in her pocket, and she knew she needed to give it back to Grayson. She was dreading the call but determined to tie up all the loose ends of her life today. Traci texted that she was held up, and Rose sighed, thinking maybe something was going her way. She wouldn't want Traci to be in the room for the call to Grayson.

Rose picked up the phone and made the dreaded call.

"Hello?" Rose closed her eyes and hoped she could make it through this call. Just because the sound of his voice brought her joy and sorrow didn't mean she couldn't do this.

"Grayson, it's me, Rose." Rose tried to put as much confidence in her voice as she could. She didn't want him to know that she spent most of last night crying, trying to think of how it all went wrong. "I realized that last night there was a disagreement between us, but I didn't want you to think that I was going to leave you, regarding Mr. Dane."

"Rose."

"Yes, it's me. I just wanted to let you know that whatever our personal disagreement is, it doesn't need to impact whatever you need to get done with Mr. Dane. I also wanted to make arrangements for when I could go ahead and either drop off or mail the ring that you gave me."

"That's it? We have a disagreement, and then the next day, we're total strangers?"

Rose took a deep breath and tried to focus on the purpose at hand. She just needed to get through this call. "I don't want to argue with you, Grayson. This is new territory for me."

"What exactly is the new part, Rose? The part where you have a fight with someone you care about? Or the part where you break up with someone and treat them like they were never important to you at all?"

Rose tapped the mute button on the phone and took three deep breaths. "I'm not running. I'm doing the right thing."

"The right thing for who?"

"Grayson. Listen to us on the phone right now. We can't even have a civil conversation. Today, Jonathan is coming over and bringing the final sale papers."

"Rose, I'm so sorry. Do you want me to come over?"

Everything in Rose wanted to tell him yes.

"Rose, I was out of line last night. You're right. I don't have kids, and I don't have the right to say anything about that either way. We can put that all behind us, and I can be there for you now."

There was such a desperate clawing feeling in Rose's chest, and she wanted to be able to say yes. She wanted to tell him she needed someone to lean on, and that right now, signing the final papers and getting the final bill of sale of this company wasn't something she wanted to face alone. The problem was some of the things that Grayson had said last night were true.

"You're right, Grayson. The kids aren't unaffected by you being around. I guess it's easy for me to go ahead and tell the kids that you're just a friend, but at the end of the day, I can't tell them how to feel about you."

Rose heard Grayson sighing on the line.

"Rose, I should have told you before. One of the reasons I went off on that tangent is because Hannah said she wanted me to go with her on the first day of school. She said the other kids were talking about how their moms and dads were going to go, and she wanted to have a mom and dad."

Rose heard the words and closed her eyes as the pain of the moment was sinking in. Had she been so blind?

"Rose?"

"I'm still here on the line. You know, I read to them every night and never once has Hannah mentioned what the other kids talk about. Not once, Grayson."

"Hannah loves you, Rose. Sometimes it's just easier to tell a stranger."

"I've got to go."

"Rose."

"Yes?"

"I want you to know I'm really sorry about last night. I know you'll think this is crazy, but I missed you."

"We just saw each other."

"I still missed you."

"I've got to go. Just email me what you want me to do about Mr. Dane and the ring, and I'll take it from there."

"I'm coming clean with Mr. Dane, and we can talk about the ring later."

Rose wanted to argue with him, but she heard the front door opening and heard Jonathan at the door.

"Jonathan is coming in now. I'll talk to you later."

Just when Rose didn't think today could become any more stressful, Jonathan walked in with the man who was about to buy her company.

CHAPTER 18

"The owner is eager to get rid of this business," Jonathan spouted. When he came around the corner he could see Rose's face, and he could tell she was not pleased.

Rose took a seat at her desk and waited for him and the buyer to come in.

Jonathan put on a bright smile.

"Rose, this is Mr. Hycam, the buyer for the business."

"Mr. Hycam." Rose shook his hand.

"Jonathan tells me you are ready to sell the business."

"I don't think I'm really ready to sell it, but I don't have a good reason to keep it," Rose said with a smile, sitting at the desk.

"Rose, I was told you were quite eager to get rid of the business."

"Well, I wouldn't say that I was eager to get rid of the business, but I will say that I don't have the financial means to keep it all going."

"I'm interested in what you could possibly say that might make me keep the business more valuable."

Rose looked at Jonathan and then back at the seller, Mr. Hycam.

"So, you wanted to keep the business?"

"Yes, it was something my husband and I built. I had hopes it would be around for when my kids were grown up."

"I don't think Mr. Hycam wants to hear about old dreams," Jonathan said as he walked in and cleared off a part of the table.

"No, on the contrary, I would like to hear about her dreams. My family came to the U.S. because of a dream, and they are important."

For a moment, there was a sense of hope that bloomed in Rose. Maybe this wasn't as over as she thought it was.

Jonathan pulled out a seat and fell into it.

"Fine, Rose. If you want to go over a dying business, then let's do that."

Rose turned to look at Mr. Hycam. "I don't know that it will make any difference, but I'd appreciate it if you'd listen to me just for a moment."

Mr. Hycam nodded.

"My name is Rose Sallow. This cleaning business was the dream of myself and my husband. We thought we were going to make this amazing business that our children would take over. It was supposed to be about what happens when you have hard work and dreams, and to let them know that things can come true. I've dedicated a lot of my time to this business, and I'm very fortunate that I have a lot of friends. They've been able to help me while I dedicated that time. Very recently, we fell upon some hard financial times, and that's why I wound up having to sell the business. So, if I had been able to raise the money or somehow save it, I wouldn't have sold this business. I would have preserved it for my kids."

Mr. Hycam looked between Rose and Jonathan and nodded.

"I commend you. I really do. I know how hard it can be when a business stops performing for you. I still think the best thing to do is to sell the business. I wanted to make sure that I was not taking from somebody who really had no say. Being able to survive a business when things become rough is also part of the business. I think that you should be very proud that you held onto your business as long as you did. But there's also a lesson, that you didn't have the money to keep it going."

Rose was disappointed. She was so sure when she had this opportunity that Mr. Hycam would change his mind.

"Thank you so much for listening to me."

"No, my dear. Thank you so much for sharing your dream with me."

"Well, it's actually for my kids and—"

Mr. Hycam laughed.

"I have five children, Miss Rose. I haven't been able to predict any of the jobs or careers that they've gone into. I do have three businesses, and I would like one of my children to take over each. Fate is going to deal me a different kind of hand. However, I will give you these words. We often build things for our children and find out we're building our own dreams we wish we would have done."

Rose signed the papers, and an hour later she was still sitting in her office, or what would be her office for just two more weeks and trying to gather her senses. She had already told Traci not to come in, and now she needed to plan for moving all of her items out of this space.

Rose grabbed her phone to call Portia.

"Portia?"

It was odd for Portia to pick up the phone on the first ring.

"Portia?"

"Rose?"

"Yeah, I was just calling you."

"I'm so sorry, I was actually calling out for somebody else."

"You don't sound great," Rose said.

"I'm here with Gloria. You know, the woman who was trying to help set up her yoga studio? It seems like at the last minute, they pulled the funding that she thought she was going to have."

Rose remembered meeting Gloria when she went to pick up her twins. It was such a shame because she knew that Gloria was very talented at relaxing people and yoga.

"So, she just lost the funding, and that's it?" Rose shook her head and sat down. It just seemed as though everything was unfair lately.

Portia sighed on the line.

"She hasn't completely lost everything. The bank is going to give her two weeks to see if she can come up with another solution. It doesn't look good. But I'm sure you didn't call to hear about Gloria's situation."

"No, but I completely understand. I just finished

signing all of the final paperwork. I wish we didn't need to sell the business."

"Oh no, girl. Do you want to get together?"

It was on the tip of Rose's tongue to say yes, they should all get together today. But she just wasn't into it. She felt as though she needed some time to think about what everybody had said because maybe they were right.

CHAPTER 19

*R*ose wasn't one to give in to self-pity moments, but this week had been all she could handle. Sitting on her couch, eating artisan carrot cake ice cream was all she could do. Fortunately, Portia had come over to sit with her on a Friday night. Traci had the kids, and this was as close as she was going to get to being down in the dumps.

"Girlfriend, cheer up. We need to look at this time as an opportunity to clean out the old closets and start anew," Portia said as she dug into her chocolate chip cookie dough ice cream.

"You know what the worst of it is? I miss him. I know after everything he said, some of it was wrong, and some of it had some little kernels of truth in it. But it doesn't even seem to matter now compared to the idea that… I miss him."

Portia stopped eating her ice cream and stared at Rose. "Well, that's a first," Portia said.

"What?"

"Do you know that when Edward passed away,

the first thing that you really talked about was how hard it was being alone? It wasn't until we were six to eight months in that you really said anything about Edward."

Rose looked at Portia as if she had lost her mind. Then when she thought about it, it became all so clear.

"Edward and I were already having all sorts of issues. He wasn't home as much as I wanted him to be. The business wasn't going as smoothly as we thought. To be honest, Edward wanted the business, but didn't want to have to work in it. I loved Edward. He could be the most amazing person. There were times when he was sweet and attentive to me. It was those times that made the other times harder to bear. Grayson, on the other hand, has always just been Grayson."

"You're probably right, but I was just noticing it took you a lot longer to get to the conclusion that you were missing Edward than it did with Grayson."

"Grayson said some pretty mean things to me," Rose said around the spoon of ice cream.

Waving her spoon in the air, Portia spoke, "The real question is, was it true?"

"You're my friend, Portia. You tell me."

"Okay, go over what you can remember he said."

"It wasn't even a week ago. Of course, I can remember it."

"I know you think that's a silly statement, but I just want you to know that I've broken up with people and then when you asked me to tell you what they said, I can only tell you what I heard."

Rose looked at Portia, and the both of them shook their heads and laughed.

"You can only say what you heard?"

Portia nodded. "The last man that I was with said he didn't think he was ready to settle down in his life. What I heard was he didn't want me, and I wasn't enough for him to do family life."

"Wow."

"So, I'm asking you whether or not you can remember what it was that Grayson said to you."

"He said that I was building a dream for the girls that maybe the girls wouldn't want."

Portia nodded.

"Is that a nod that you agree with him or that you understand the statement?" Rose asked.

"It's a nod that I agree with him."

Rose flopped back onto the couch and started eating her ice cream again. "Fine, maybe that's true. He also said that I was putting in all this work, saying that it was for the kids, so I wouldn't have to focus on me."

Portia whistled. "I'm not touching that one with a ten-foot pole."

Rose sighed. "You don't have to. I already did, and he was right. It was just so much easier to focus on the girls than it was to focus on myself. I think the other part of that was if I had to focus on myself, then I'd have to think about what my relationship was like with Edward before he died."

"Was it so bad?" Portia asked.

"What Edward and I had wasn't bad. It's just it wasn't the relationship that I thought I was getting into when I got married."

"And you thought…?"

"I thought it was going to be us against the world. But it turned out to be me staying home and

Edward going out to try to conquer the world. Don't get me wrong, it wasn't a bad life, and he was a good man, but we weren't partners, and I wanted that. Grayson made me feel like we were partners."

"Rose, you are the most responsible and giving person that I know. I'm always amazed that we're friends and that we've been together so long because I know I can be single-minded and difficult. You see the best in everyone else, and you give the most of yourself no matter what. However, there is something to be said for the idea that you always put yourself last. You're an amazing mother and an outstanding friend, but you may not be taking care of yourself as much as you should."

Rose kept eating her ice cream. It wasn't like she hadn't thought of the same things that Portia had said. When Rose thought about how Grayson had said he missed her, it made something inside her stomach curl up and twist. He had been willing to put himself out there, even after the argument. The night was spent in laughter, ice cream, and old movies, but in the back of Rose's head, she was wondering if she made an epic mistake with Grayson by not talking to him.

Determined to do the right thing by Grayson, Rose called Mr. Dane's office to find out he was going to be going to a fundraiser at a commercial event in town. She dressed in a black pants suit, feeling armed and empowered. Rose arrived at the gala and used Mr. Dane as the person she was there to see. The room was filled with Inheritance Bay's up-and-coming, ready to open their wallets to give to a good cause.

Rose looked for Grayson, hoping she could find him before he confessed to Mr. Dane. So many people stopped her to say hello, but none of them were Grayson. Rose thought for sure that Grayson would come to this event to talk to Mr. Dane. It was such a crush, though she wasn't sure she'd be able to find herself after a little while. Then, out of nowhere, she heard her name.

"Rose?"

To Rose's surprise, it was Gloria Danvers. This was a completely different Gloria. In a black sheath dress, they outlined the shapely figure and lean muscles. She looked like a siren who was walking on the land.

"Gloria?"

"I know, I know. I clean up well. That's all there is to it," Gloria said as she came closer and pulled Rose into an embrace.

"I didn't know you'd be here," Rose said.

"I was hoping I wouldn't have to be here, to be quite honest. I don't know if you heard, but the funding for my yoga studio was pulled at the last minute. I was hoping that I would be here at this fundraiser and be able to sell someone on the benefits of yoga for children."

"I'm sure if they had ever seen you manage a class, they wouldn't even hesitate to give you the money."

"You're too kind. So, I know why I'm here. Why are you here?"

"I'm looking for Grayson Chance. Do you know him?"

Gloria laughed. "I would say that everybody here knows him. He's the one who put together this fundraiser."

Rose nodded, and suddenly it all made sense. "Have you seen him?"

"Yes, I think that's him over there by the fountain. I met him earlier, and he's with a woman. I think her name is Sheila."

Rose turned toward the fountain and sure enough, she saw Grayson with a beautiful brunette woman. The woman's hair fell midway down her back, and she looked as though she just stepped off the pages of a magazine. A few moments later, Mr. Dane joined them, patting both of them on their back. Rose thought, I guess Sheila changed her mind. Seeing how easily they talked and walked with one another pierced daggers in her heart.

Gloria started to talk again, but Rose couldn't really hear her words. All her attention was transfixed on the couple in front. She was happy she didn't get to Mr. Dane first, because she would have only embarrassed herself, or even worse, messed up everything for Grayson. Realizing that Grayson had already replaced her, Rose's only thought was wondering how she could get out of this room without being seen.

Rose had just reoriented herself so she could find an exit when she took one last glance over at Grayson, and that was when their eyes locked. He stopped walking and turned toward Rose. It was then he must have felt the hand on his shoulder of what Rose could only presume was Sheila. When he turned to say something to her, Rose took that time to make her getaway.

When Rose made it outside, there didn't seem to be enough air for her, and she noticed that her eyes were starting to water. So that was Sheila. Rose should have known that he would improvise to make sure he could get the house and the home that he's always wanted. It was only the drop of rain that made her aware that she had stopped walking. She put her hand on the ring on her finger and took it off. It wasn't real anyway. Maybe it was for the best. Maybe Sheila came to a new decision now that she had spent some time away from Grayson. Rose wasn't angry with Sheila; in fact, she was happy for Grayson and hoped he found everything he was looking for.

When Rose arrived at her house, she heard the twins and Traci. She didn't want them to see her the way she was now. She went to her bedroom and closed the door. Rose knew she should have been beyond happy for Grayson, and she was, but she was sad for what she'd lost.

The thing that made this the worst was that she couldn't tell anybody. She hadn't told her friends that there was a fake engagement. She had never worn the ring anywhere, so now she had a pain that she couldn't tell anyone without seeming like she was lying. Grayson was right. It was always easier to focus on other things and other people than to focus on what her needs were.

The thought that she and Grayson would never be helped her realize that she had neglected herself so much that she had probably lost one of the best things that she found in her life. Seeing him in Sheila's arms made her wish him nothing but happiness. Rose grabbed a pillow and curled into a ball. She would get past this. It didn't feel like she would now, but she knew she would be able to survive it. She didn't know how long she had laid in her bed, but just when she was about to get up, the phone in her pants started pinging. With her luck, Gloria had called Portia, and now Portia wanted to know how she was. Prepared to get some more artisan ice cream, she opened her phone.

It was Grayson.

WHERE ARE YOU? WHY ARE YOU CONSTANTLY LEAVING ME?

Each word was a gift, and Rose was loathed to touch them for fear she might delete the words from the man she loved.

YOU WERE BUSY.

SHEILA WANTED TO MEET YOU.

WHAT?

I NEED YOU.

"Rose?"

Rose screamed and sat up on her bed, only to see Traci at the door.

"You know, only the guilty scream like that."

"I don't know what you're talking about."

"If I had to take a guess, I'd bet you were texting Grayson just now," Traci said with a smile.

Rose threw herself back onto the bed and groaned. "What is wrong with me?"

"Well, I'm not a real doctor, and I can't even tell you I'm really good in this particular area, but if I had to take a guess, I'd say you're probably in love with him."

"Don't say that."

"Don't you want to be in love with him?"

Rose curled onto her side. "It's so complicated."

"Ah, so you have done something that you don't want to talk about."

"I didn't say that."

"No, you didn't. But you didn't say you hadn't done that, either."

Rose sat up and looked at Traci.

"I want you to remember that you are supposed to be my friend and not his. That no matter how crazy I sound, you are always supposed to say, you go girl."

Traci smiled and nodded.

"I think I do love him, but I broke up with him."

"You go girl."

Rose smiled and went on. "Then tonight, I tried to do something to make it better, and I saw him with another woman and so I left."

"You really go, girl?"

"Then he texts me to say that he misses me, and he needs me and that the woman with him was there to meet me, too."

"Oh girl, you have really gone."

Traci and Rose looked at one another and then started to laugh.

"What am I going to do?"

"Answer your phone."

Rose looked at the blinking phone. She'd gotten three other text messages. She picked her phone up and read them.

I MISS YOU. I MISS THE TWINS. SECOND GRADE READERS ARE HARD TO READ. NOT HAVING YOU WITH ME MADE ME FEEL EMPTY.

Rose placed the phone next to her, facing down.

"And?"

"I have no idea what to do."

"The first thing you need to do is be selfish. What do you want to do?"

"I want to tell him to come over so we can make this better."

Traci pulled Rose into her arms and gave her a big hug.

"You go girl."

CHAPTER 20

The twins were running around like it was a madhouse, and Grayson was on his way. As soon as Rose told Hannah, she jumped up for joy and congratulated her on a good decision.

Now Rose was looking at the door as if it were a living thing. Could she do this? Was she sure? Then the doorbell rang, and she just stared at it. She could move, she could. Then a blur went past her, and Hannah looked out the window on the side of the door.

"It's Grayson!" The twins screamed and scrambled to open the door. He was swamped, and he hadn't even stepped into the house.

"Hello, little women. I come bearing gifts." He picked up a brown bag next to him and gave it to Hannah.

"He brought us gifts! Woo hoo!"

Inside was a wind-up dog that Anna thought was adorable. The other gift was a baby doll dressed as a ballerina that said phrases when you pulled the string. The kids were ecstatic. Then he looked up, and Rose held her breath.

"You look amazing," he said.

It was so high school, but Rose ran her hand through her hair and smiled.

"It was nothing. I'm just wearing jeans and a t-shirt." She could have told him how she spent the last couple of hours picking this simple outfit, so she didn't look desperate, but Rose was going to keep that to herself. Right now, she was trying to move without tripping over her feet.

"You look yummy, too." Did his hair get darker and shinier? Was there some way he had put more waves in his hair? The jeans still outlined a muscular man who kept himself together. Then it dawned on Rose what she just said.

"I-I mean you look good, too."

Grayson watched the twins run into their room and Traci told them to slow down. Then he walked up to Rose and stopped a foot in front of her.

"Do I look carrot cake kind of yummy? Or just like ice cream yummy?"

"Carrot cake is asking an awful lot. If it's any consolation, I'm going to give you a cupcake yummy."

"The real question is, is yummy going to really cut it?"

"What are you trying to do?" she asked.

"Fix something that happened in the past and make sure that we're good for the future."

"I think we need to slow things down and really make sure we know what we're doing. Communication is the key."

"I agree with you. So, let's start this the right way. Can I have that ring back?"

The smile on Rose's face started to falter. She knew this was the right thing to do. Even if she had feelings for him, he might not be ready to marry her.

"Of course," Rose said. She took the ring off and dropped it into his extended hand. Then Grayson pocketed the ring and dropped to one knee.

"So, I was wondering if you would take some time and invest in this cause I'm working for."

Rose could barely contain her smile. "What's the cause?"

"It's the 'show Rose Sallow how much she's loved' cause. I know way more worthy people may come by, but none of them will be more devoted and committed to this cause than me."

"You know, I think Rose was looking for a fundraiser just like you, so you're in luck."

Grayson reached into his other pocket and pulled out a ring case. When he opened it, inside was a ring and a modest diamond set between two opals.

"I got it on the good authority that you like opals, and I thought I needed to bring my A-game to this merger."

"I see the ring. I see the man on his knee. Is there something you are getting at?" Rose said as tears began to fall down her face.

"Rose Sallow, do me the honor of getting to know me so that we can spend the rest of our lives together so I can show you how much I love you."

"Yes! Yes! Silly man. I do, I will! Get up!"

Grayson smiled and then reached for her hand. He slid the ring on it and then stood up.

"Grayson, in case you didn't know, I love you. Now kiss me."

Grayson kissed Rose. To make the moment perfect, Rose heard the twins behind her.

"Thank goodness they are going to be friends. Now our first day of school is going to be perfect."

EPILOGUE

C at-cow.

"I'd probably sell one or both of them to get the money for my place."

Go into downward dog.

"I can see how my old coworkers would think I'm crazy trying to build a life that isn't a rat race."

Gloria Danvers felt the bun on her head starting to fall, and she silently huffed under her breath. She wasn't surprised that something else in her life wasn't going right. Then her phone rang, and it was the ringtone of her ex–Davis. She just gave up trying to find some inner calm because her old life was calling her. This was how it always happened. When Gloria was trying to get away from the old and do something new, a barrier would show up. So many times, she had tried to leave the finance world. Oh, she was great at it. She could manage money like no one could. Her commissions were through the roof, and her life was fast and ultimately meaningless.

It wasn't that finance was meaningless, it was just

the stress that had cost her a dream that was dear to her. That moment had been a turning point in her life, and she had never looked back. Her brother saved her and brought her to Inheritance Bay. At first, Gloria thought that he had brought her to a place to die. Who saves themselves from loneliness by going to a small town? She used to think that before she met the people of Inheritance Bay.

The phone rang again, and again Gloria prepared to ignore Davis's call. Then she listened to the ringtone and realized it was Portia. Gloria sprinted from her bedroom to the living room until she had the phone in hand. Portia was the one who was looking into new ways for Gloria to get the funding for the studio. Gloria thought the funding had been secured with her bank in Boston, but at the last minute, they called and said it was too risky to use her investment account as collateral. If she liquidated it, then they would consider the cash as collateral instead. She had been devastated, and it had all seemed so unfair and sudden.

Portia was certain they could find a local bank to help them out. Portia had gone out of her way to help Gloria. She was sure she would be able to find another backer. She had even invited her to a fundraiser held by Grayson Chance. A lot of people were interested, but they wanted her to come back to them when she had been in business for six months. Gloria smiled and took their names and numbers, but she had been dying on the inside. There would be no six months if she couldn't get the funding to open her doors.

Gloria picked up the phone and waited anxiously. "Portia?"

"Hi, Gloria. I told you I would get back to you, and I wanted to make good on that promise."

Gloria heard the defeat in Portia's voice and sat down. "I take it from your tone, no luck."

"I'm sorry, Gloria, I'm not sure what's going on. I didn't want to say this before, but I think we're at the point where I need to..."

"Yes?"

"It just seems really odd the way the funding fell apart, and if I didn't know any better, I would have thought that maybe someone called in a favor."

"What?"

"I guess what I'm trying to ask you, Gloria, is do you know anybody in Boston who would have wanted you to fail? Who had enough pull with a bank?"

Gloria wanted to tell her how crazy that sounded, but then Davis Lorel came to mind. An investment banker who moved millions and was able to give people the inside track once or twice, if that was what business called for. It wasn't beyond him.

"I'm not sure, but I can check."

"I'm at my wit's end right now, but of course, I'll keep looking."

"No, Portia, I want you to know you have done more than what I could have expected."

"If anything, else comes up, you know I'll bring it to you."

"Thanks, Portia."

Gloria hung up the phone, and she could feel the anger building in her toward Davis. Then she stopped herself. Maybe it wasn't Davis. Maybe she was just looking for an easy target. There was only one way to find out. Gloria hit number three on speed dial and waited.

"Hello, Gloria."

There was that smug tone that said he knew. If practicing yoga had taught her anything, it was to be patient.

"Davis, you called me."

"I wanted to see how things were going and if you were able to open up that yoga studio yet?"

"As far as I know, things are right on schedule."

"Really?"

"No one has told me any different."

"You didn't get a call from the bank in Boston?

"Why would I get such a call, Davis?" Gloria said in a sweet, saccharine voice.

"Um, well, I don't know. I was just thinking with the economy changing these days and—"

"And the good old boy network is still in place. You wanted to make sure that your buddy had called and told me that he was going to revoke my loan unless I cashed out all my investments."

She heard Davis sigh on the other end. "Stop this foolishness and come home."

Gloria closed her eyes and thought about how once upon a time she would have begged to hear those words.

"I've made a new home now, Davis."

"We can try again."

Gloria sat down and wrapped her arms around herself. Davis knew all the words to say. He was a master of words. It was one of the reasons she originally fell in love with him. Now he was using those words like a fine-tuned weapon.

"Davis, I can't be in that world anymore."

Davis snorted on the other line. "I can wait, Gloria. You may think you can't be in this world anymore, but you're going to find this is the only world that's for you."

"Davis, I—"

"Have a nice vacation, Gloria, because that is all that is in Inheritance Bay. A vacation. I'll be here when you come to your senses and come home."

"Then you'll be waiting a mighty long time."

"And what will you do without the money to open your studio?"

"I'll find it, Davis, and I'll make this work."

"You're being stubborn."

"You're not even thinking about me. All of this is about your image and how it looked to the partners. It's been three years. Certainly, you've been able to find another up-and-coming star in three years."

"It's not like that, Gloria. I want what's best for us. I won't deny that the partnership would look better if we were together. It's a factor, but not the only one."

"Well, that world is over for me."

"We will see. Have fun looking for your funding, Gloria."

Gloria hung up the phone and then tossed it across the room. She didn't want him to be right. She didn't want to have to go back to the thing that she knew. Her brother was offering to help her, but he had just opened up his own business, as well. She wouldn't bankrupt his dream trying to fund hers. Just as she was going to her room to try and find some peace she heard a text message come in. It was from Portia.

I THINK I MAY HAVE AN IDEA.

~

If you enjoyed The Bachelor's Wife and want more, "The Loner's Wife" (Gloria and Reid's Story) is available now! You'll get more of Grayson and Rose's wedding plans, and you'll get to see why Gloria walked away from her career and why Reid is afraid to love anyone.

If you Scroll on, you can read the
first chapter of The Loner's Wife. I
hope you'll give it a chance!
THE END (…for now)

Inheritance Bay saved Gloria Danvers's life. Okay, it wasn't like it took up arms and defended her. It also didn't magically heal her with its on the Bay community. What it did for her was it gave her a place where she could go to recuperate. If it hadn't been for Inheritance Bay, Gloria would have still been stuck in Boston, mourning a loss that she could never get back.

After six months of just existing, her brother Jack showed up, packed her condo, and brought her to Inheritance Bay. For the first month, Gloria didn't really notice she was in a different place. In fact, nothing mattered to Gloria. The only thing that seemed to break through her depression was running into a little girl named Priscilla. Priscilla lived next door to Jack. Her mother, Joan, worked as the lunch matron in the school. One day, when Priscilla was trying to touch her toes, she just toppled over. Gloria was looking out the window waiting for what she didn't know but she had made it her habit to look out of her window every day. When she saw Priscilla topple over it caught her eye. Gloria was depressed, but she would never turn away from a child.

"Are you hurt?"

Startled the little girl yelped. Gloria stopped where she stood and held her hands in front of her.

"I'm not trying to hurt you. I saw you from the window and thought you might be hurt."

Priscilla threw back her straight black hair and blew the bangs out of her eyes.

"My mom says you are the woman whose heart is hurt."

Gloria wasn't surprised. In a town like Inheritance Bay, any newcomer would be noticed, classified, and talked about.

"I'm Jack's sister."

"Older sister or younger sister?" Priscilla asked looking at Gloria with curiosity.

"Younger."

Priscilla nodded. "Then it's good your brother went to get you."

Gloria wasn't so sure, but she didn't disagree with her neighbor. Trying to deflect the girl from digging anymore into what was the shambles of a life Gloria pointed to the ground.

"What were you trying to do?"

The girl just plopped to the ground. "I am in a class at school, and I have to do looking down dog."

Gloria smiled at the girl.

"You mean upside-down dog?"

The girl nodded. "Yes, that."

"Why?"

The girl looked at her feet and then let out a big sigh. "I'm fat."

Gloria looked at the young girl and wasn't sure she heard correctly.

"That can't be."

The girl looked up with tears in her eyes. "At school, everyone can do this but me, so the kids say I'm too fat."

Gloria looked at the girl and for the first time in six months, she felt something.

"Look, I happen to know how to do Yoga. I can show you how to do it. You are very close."

The girl looked hopeful, and it was that day that Gloria found her purpose. She would be a yoga teacher for school-age kids. Ever since that day Gloria had worked part-time at the school and gotten certified as a yoga instructor for kids. Everything seemed to be in place until she decided to open a yoga school and then she looked at her finances.

A lot of her money was in long-term investments that if she took it out too soon she might pay more in taxes than she could really afford. Then she looked at her savings and when she went to pull the money out Davis called her and said they would have to settle on the amount. The account was in both of their names. Gloria thought they would split 50/50 but Davis said his expenses were much higher after she abandoned him, and he would need 75% of the fund. He would release it if she would come back to Boston and to the finance firm, they both use to work at. The leave she had taken was indefinite because the firm knew how well she worked but it wouldn't last forever.

Gloria had broken up with Davis for three years. She had taken the leave a year after her breakup with Davis. Jack had rescued her after she sulked in her condo for six months after that and her she was.

When Gloria told him she had made up her decision and she was not going back Davis said they would have to settle the money issue in court. Miraculously they couldn't get a court date that wasn't less than a year out.

So much for wanting to support a loved one, Gloria thought. That was how she found herself sitting in the perfect town of Inheritance Bay with less than a week to come up with 150k or a bank that would give her a loan for the amount. At this point, neither one of them seemed likely.

Then Portia called and said she had an idea. Gloria was nervous because Portia wouldn't tell her a thing about this idea, instead, Portia asked her to meet up for brunch on a Saturday. Now there was no doubt that Portia had been a help beyond words, but this type of ambiguity was setting Gloria's senses on alert. It was Portia, someone she trusted. It wasn't like she was Davis but still Gloria was uneasy with the cloak and dagger.

To be honest Gloria could probably attest her feelings to the fundraiser. She hated having to go to the fundraiser and pitch to people. It was too much like her old life. The problem with that was Gloria was able to pitch without a problem and she fit right into that role as if she had never left. She hadn't been good enough to get funding but it had made her uncomfortable enough to make her not want to deal with large crowds.

The good part was, she would never have to see Grayson Chance again. Gloria was sure Portia would come with her upbeat attitude because she wasn't ready to admit defeat, but Gloria was close. Close but not close enough to tell Portia no about coming here today.

"Gloria!" Portia smiled and she almost looked relieved. Gloria has to work on hiding her emotions better if she was so transparent Portia doubted she would come to the breakfast.

Gloria stood up and hugged Portia. A carafe of orange juice and some biscuits are on the table. I think it's refreshing that the place gives you real butter and some fattening foods for the world that wants to enjoy their days instead of counting calories.

"Are we having the farmers special today?" Portia asked.

Anyone who knows Gloria knows she likes to eat. When Portia makes the suggestion it actually relaxes Gloria. She never felt like she had to put up pretense around Portia and that is just one more thing she likes about being around her.

"You got here first. Were you eager to see me," Portia asked as she settled at the table.

"I'm always anxious to see you. I like you, Portia, you are what you say you are and I feel totally comfortable," Gloria said.

"I'm surprised at the fundraiser you didn't meet a nice guy," Portia said.

"Meet a guy while I'm going through this?"

"I'm not saying that the event was for meeting a guy but I'm saying there were a lot of guys that were interested or at the very least who asked me about you," Portia said wiggling her eyebrows.

"Well, they are just going to have to wait until I have the yoga studio up," Gloria said as she slathered butter onto a biscuit.

"You know I admire your focus to start over and get the studio up, but don't you ever wish for …."

Gloria put her biscuit down and looked at Portia. One of the things she thought was such an oddity about Portia was her optimism.

"Are you asking me if I miss being in a relationship? The answer would be no. Besides I realized that before I could be in a relationship with someone else I needed to be okay being in a relationship with me.'

Portia laughed. "If you spent any more time with yourself alone we'd all think you had gotten married to yourself."

"Ha, ha," Gloria groaned.

Gloria heard Portia but Gloria was still a hot mess. She wouldn't want to bring a man into her life who would have to deal with her past and Davis. It wouldn't be fair to them.

"Anyway, Grayson said the fundraising party went really well. He was really impressed with you. He said a lot of people commented on your professional demeanor.

"It's a shame a lot of them did not comment on how they would be willing to invest upfront in my studio."

"I think that Grayson may be able to still help us," Portia said.

Gloria wasn't sure what Portia thought Grayson

could do, but she was out of options, but she was willing to hear just about anything.

"I'm not sure what Grayson can do at this point, but I'd be willing to hear whatever he had to say."

Portia put her plate on the side, and she folded her hands in front of her on the table.

"I'm so glad that you're so open because he'll be here in a minute.

"Excuse me?" Gloria looked at Portia as if she'd lost her mind then Gloria looked at herself. Her hair was in a high ponytail. She had on her stressed jeans and her black sneakers that had paint stains on them. She wasn't even going to think about the college tee shirt she had on.

"Please tell me that you're kidding, Portia," Gloria whispered.

"Sorry, I'm not. Remember, this is about the studio, not about being mad at Portia. Grayson is looking for help for one of his brothers."

"His brother went to private yoga sessions?"

Portia's smile became twice as large, and she stood up to wave to what Gloria could only be Grayson.

"No, his brother doesn't need yoga sessions. His brother needs a financial planner. Before you lose your mind as the man is walking toward us, I'd like you to know that his brother needs a lot of help and Grayson needed someone he could trust."

Gloria slumps in the chair and looked in disbelief at Portia. "How could you tell him?"

"How could I not when you were sitting here in all of your dreams are on the line?"

Gloria pulled on the smile that she's used so often

before that she swore she would never have to use it again. In truth, this was the problem no matter how far Gloria seemed to try to get away from it, she was always being pulled back into the finance world. That was the world that had taken something from her it could never replace. Gloria fortified herself. She'd listen to Grayson and smile accordingly and then send him to Davis as a consolation prize. There was no way she'd do this.

Grayson Chance was eye candy at any age. He was 5'10" with dark wavy hair and a smile that made everyone feel like a long-lost friend.

"Gloria, it's good to see you again," Grayson said.

"Sorry for the dress down, but Portia just told me that you were coming."

Grayson grinned at Portia. "I guess this meeting wasn't as planned as I thought it was. While we were doing the fundraising I was telling Portia how my brother is an entrepreneur. He finds startups, early invests, and sometimes if he likes the company keeps 10% here and there. It used to be that I would look at his investments and books every quarter, but my brother has been busy this last year and his investments have tripled. I don't know if you are aware, but I'm engaged to Rose Sallow. Which means I'm being trained by the twins on all the things I need to know while we plan for the wedding."

With a happy couple, twins, and a wedding, there was no way that Gloria would be able to help him. Gloria looked at Portia who was still smiling. Gloria discreetly kicked Portia under the table, and Portia reached out to pat her hand.

"I don't know if I can help you."

"Well, it's not really me that needs the help. It's my brother, Reid."

Gloria glanced at Porsche and then back at Grayson. She could see that neither one of them was going to make this easy for her.

"Listen, I hear you, but I just think that maybe you could find somebody else who would be better. On top of everything else, you know that I'm really dedicated to getting my studio up and running. I just don't see how there would be time —"

Grayson held up his hand. "I know, I know what you're going to say. Portia was clear when she said that you never do financial work and that it's no longer even in your future plans. I'm going to be just as honest with you as Portia was with me. I want to make sure that my brother doesn't get taken advantage of and frankly, he's away too often on his entrepreneurial whatevers in order to make sure that doesn't happen. I don't want you to stay with him forever. I just want you to get him set up so that he can have a plan at least that he can give to someone to help him manage his finances. I'd also want you to go to maybe one or two of the places that have come up recently just to look at them to make sure that they are sound investments. Before you hand it off."

"Grayson, I know a lot of competent financial planners."

Just then the waiter shows up and delivers the morning specials to everyone. Grayson and Gloria both look at Portia.

"You were both talking, and we have to eat," Portia said trying to defend her action of ordering the special for everyone.

Gloria stared at Portia and thought this was probably the only time she wasn't thinking about food. Gloria felt really bad for Grayson. He seemed like he wanted to do right by his brother. She also knew that Portia was trying to help, but neither one of them understood why she had walked away from finance. But if there were some small slivers of hope that her going back to finance would help her to get her studio, she might do it. Right now, for Gloria, the numbers just didn't add up.

Grayson took a bite, but it appeared to be in everything omelet with some Texas French toast on the side.

"Listen, Gloria, I know that money is an issue and I want you to know that I can go ahead and pay for the time you'll be helping my brother."

Gloria, heard the words coming out of his mouth but knew he didn't really understand the kind of money she needed. He had done the fundraiser, but he had let her negotiate the amount with funders. While Gloria was very impressed with the people who came to his fundraiser, she still didn't think he understood what it took to get a business up and to have three years of financing in the bank. Then she thought about what it would mean to have to go ahead and go over financial planning every day with his brother and try not to remember all the reasons why she left it, she wasn't sure she could do that.

Gloria's strategy was pretty simple. All of this could come to it amicable stop if she just gave him a number that there was no way that he could meet. She didn't have to wonder what that number was. She could give him the number that she'd been looking for the last month and a half.

"What kind of investments does he have?"

"He has domestic and international accounts. I'd like for him to have a plan that he understands but one that he can hand to someone else if need be but still be aware of the schedule," Grays said. "I'll admit it's hard to pin Reid down and even harder when you're his brother. I'm open to getting a copy of the plan when its done but I need to get him to see it and be a part of the process without me present every step of the way."

"That seems like a win-win situation so you'll know someone will benefit from the work you do," Portia said. Gloria wasn't sure if she wanted to agree with her or strangle her.

"Grayson, I was serious when I told you I know someone who can do this for you."

Grayson nodded sagely and pushed his plate aside while he folds his hands in front of him.

"Well, let's get to the heart of the matter then. How about I offer you 250,000 and you take care of everything?

That was when Gloria looked at Portia and asked.

"Is this for real?"

Portia smiled and nodded. Gloria faced Grayson and pasted on a smile.

"If the number holds and I can get 50% upfront, you've got a deal."

Grayson smiled.

"I deliver it all by five today. I know where you live so I'm not worried about flight risk." With that Grayson pulled his plate in front of him and ate with gusto. Gloria wouldn't even be able to remember what was on her plate, just that she was going back to the fire.

~

IF YOU ENJOYED THAT SAMPLE, "The Loner's Wife" is available now at your favorite storefront!